KINGSLEY L. DENNIS

MUNDUS GRUNDY

&

THE IGNOBLE GOBLIN INVASION

BEAUTIFUL TRAITOR BOOKS

CONTENTS

To

The Invisible One
(for being invisible)

CHAPTER ONE
A DANGEROUS MISSION

Mundus Grundy crept low through the undergrowth; his purple felt hat perched on his head keeping him warm in the human night. Mundus peered ahead, his deep-set wise old brown eyes searching and scanning the terrain. His laugh wrinkles were strained and not laughing but looking the full 444 years. He stopped and scratched his bushy white beard. Somewhere there was an itch. If only he could find out exactly where? Mundus and his fellow gnomes were creeping through the middle of the darkest night. Yet for them, it was as if they were peering at a dusky deep-orange sunset for gnomes see differently, you see? Only owls, it is said, are able to see similar to how gnomes see in the Third Realm. And owls, like many of the creatures living in the realm inhabited by humans, treat gnomes as their friends. After all, it is the gnomes, or woodchucks as they are sometimes called, who take care of Mother Nature when humans are sleeping. Yet if a human ever comes across a gnome by accident…well, you can be sure that the gnome will end up in their garden as just another ornament. This is exactly how gnome parents scare their little gnomies when they are young – *"You'll end up a stone-gnome in a big fellow's garden!"* For this is true. Let it be known, here and now, that if any human clamps eyes upon a gnome, the gnome immediately turns to stone. All gnomes shudder in their brown felt boots when they think of this. Perhaps the only thing worse than being a stone-gnome is to be snotted on by a snotgurgle. But these days snotgurgles are few and far between, having been banished from the Second Realm for their wickedness. They now hide deep away in mountains of the Third Realm, out of sight of humans. Some of them are known to live in both the Ural and the Carpathian Mountains. If gnomes are wise, they never go there.

And so, Mundus Grundy stepped softly, swiftly, and stealthily through the overgrown grass of a graveyard at the back of a small church. Behind him followed his best friend and deputy, Baga Gheet, who was simply called Baga by his friends. And behind Baga tip-toed the inquisitive figure of Fender Tart, the young apprentice gnome rescuer. For the gnomes were on a rescue mission to find one of their own lost brothers – stone-gnomed in the Third Realm. Both Baga and Fender, with their trademark red pointy hats perched on their heads, and concentration etched on their faces, hung upon every word of Mundus. For Mundus, you see, was not only the oldest amongst them, and supposedly one of the wisest gnomes in all of Grundusland – he was also said to be the most cunning woodchuck ever to don the purple hat of King. Mundus was even reported to have battled against a snotgurgle in the Urals and escaped from his foul breath and stinking snot. A gnome to be reckoned with, for sure!

"What can you see, Mundus?" asked Baga from behind.

"Bother!" called back Mundus in a gruff voice.

"What kind of bother?" asked Baga.

"Bothering botherness – and lots of it!" The King of Gnomes grumbled to himself. It was not his preferred choice of activity to be out in the cold dead of night sneaking through 'big fellow' territory. His warm bed back at Grundy Castle would be missing him. Yet duty was duty – and gnomes were known for their duty, if nothing else.

Mundus crept low and came to a standstill as he approached what appeared to be a largish hole in the ground – and the hole was seemingly getting bigger. They could hear a horrible low moan drifting up from the hole and it hung in the air like the sound of an injured badger.

"What's that?" Baga peered from behind Mundus's rounded back. Baga had a circular face and looked more childlike than Mundus, although he himself was 399 years old. Baga had sprouting on his face a slightly smaller beard than Mundus, and his eyes had a determined look. Gnomes are well-known to be inquisitive and somewhat fearless – to a degree

"It's a leak, of course. And it's nasty," said Mundus. "They're getting worse each time. I wonder what can be causing these sudden leaks and energy blockages."

"Mmm…more chaos for the big fellows," replied Baga, referring to the humans.

"Well, those big fellows have had it coming to them with all of their trickster ways and dealings," said Mundus with a shake of his head.

"What's that moaning?" called Fender Tart from the back, his voice high and squeaky like a field mouse. Fender was just a young woodchuck of 255 years, still somewhat untrained in the gnomish arts – which meant he was still a little under-serious for major gnomish tasks of great importance. However, it was time to train Fender in the art of Third Realm entering, maintenance, and – when necessary – gnome rescue. And, like an eager student, Fender had read, from back to front, the whole **GRALE** manual (Gnome **R**escue **A**nd **L**iberation **E**xpedition). Most gnomes refer to such a rescue as the 'Holy Grale.' Fender was as ready as any young gnome would be ready, to rescue a fellow woodchuck who had been spied by human eyes while on duty in the Third Realm. Turning to stone, he was quite sure, was not a nice thing. What if one had an itch that just had to be scratched? No, being a stone-gnome was not a pleasant state indeed!

Fender was peering past Mundus and Baga towards where the hole was spreading upon the ground. The deep-orange haze of the night added to the eeriness of the sound, as nearby trees bent and croaked in the wind. Strange and odd things had been happening in parts of the Third Realm. There had been small earthquakes in a village called Dolphinholme that caused the bridge to collapse, scaring the inhabitants half to death. The local villagers couldn't decide if a gas pipe had burst or if strange creatures were burrowing underneath the village. And a local reservoir nearby had cracked and flooded the only school for miles around. All the children were happy that school had been cancelled for a week, but the adults were furious – they didn't know what to do with their children or how to entertain them! Things were seemingly a little off-kilter.

"'Tis not natural wind is that," squeaked Fender. All three gnomes tilted their heads to one side and listened quietly.

Mundus sniffed a few times. "Odd smell too. This is going to be a dangerous mission, I fear." He mumbled in a low voice, catching the eye of both the other gnomes. All stood still for a moment as if in frozen expectation.

"Blahhhh…umphh," roared Mundus as he lurched and poked Baga in his little potbelly. Baga fell back with an "eeek," knocking over Fender who stood behind him. Both gnomes lay splatted on the floor with eyes wide open and their podgy round noses twitching in surprise.

"Nobby-gnomes!" called out Mundus. The laughter lines on his aged face were jiggling about like eels. "My, my, my," said Mundus, shaking his head. "You lot seem about as alert as gnome-stools." Baga and Fender slowly scrambled up and with squinted eyes looked down at their feet in embarrassment, before each of them broke out into broad grins.

"Smecker!" Baga giggled, his round face curling up into a wrinkled ball.

"Gnome-head!" squeaked Fender.

Mundus suddenly jumped into action and began scrambling past the gravestones, looking for something. It had to be nearby, and it was time to find it fast, in double gnome-time. Mundus knew he had to fix the problem before the gnome rescue could go ahead. These increasing instances of sudden holes appearing in the fabric of the Third Realm were causing great concern to gnomes and could affect the stability of the Three Realms. If the problem could not be fixed soon it would mean more big fellows – the humans – becoming dizzy and sick. More than that, it would mean the earth would begin to shake. I mean, really begin to shake. The three gnomes, dressed in their trademark blue smocks, green trousers, and brown felt boots, all scurried around the back of the graveyard. They had to make sure that they dodged the growing vortex-hole that was moaning low and deep. And there it was, next to a certain Mrs. Ethel Jones's gravestone.

"Those daft big fellows have gone and moved the stones!" exclaimed Mundus. He shook his head in disbelief. "I need a pile of stones, and quickly." Baga and Fender silently scurried away to find some suitable stones. Mundus took a strange metal instrument from his tool kit that was attached to a leather belt around his waist. It looked somewhat like a silver-colored protractor with an eyepiece attached to one end. Mundus held the device up to his eyes and scanned the graveyard. He then pointed over to a corner in the graveyard and made a strange code signal with his hands. Baga immediately changed direction, with Fender following behind him, wide-eyed and attentive. Obviously, Fender had little idea of what was going on.

"What are we doing?" asked Fender in a hushed voice.

"We need to stabilize the vortex," replied Baga authoritatively. Then turning to face Fender he straightened up tall – which really wasn't that tall – and raised his podgy little hand. "Let me explain the gnome procedure." Baga cleared his throat. "We have a gnome-situation here. There's a rip in the energy fabric of the Third Realm – gnome-me how it happened! Anyways, we've got to fix the leak in gnome-quick time. And first we need a circle of stones to do this – so hop to it double smartish, my little gnomie brother."

Fender did a little jiggle on the spot. "Yes, Baga Gheet, sir!" He scampered away to look for stones in a corner of the graveyard.

"Gnome-head," whispered Baga under his breath.

"Over here." Mundus called softly to Baga and Fender as they approached carrying stones that were almost twice their size.

"How many stones this time, Mundus?" asked Baga, a little out of breath.

"Oh, half a dozen less than two dozen," replied Mundus, as he tugged at his long white beard in thought. Fender came trotting up behind with another large stone, balanced against his forehead and blocking his sight.

Gnomes are extremely efficient when they want to be. In fact, it's their nature to be workers, and not to laze around like ragamuffins or like the big fellows in their warm homes in front of their color-boxes.

Several stone trips later, Baga and Fender were standing next to Mundus with their hands on their hips. Mundus was peering at the circle of stones arranged around the vortex-hole, which had now stopped growing.

"The whole matrix grid here is completely screwy." Mundus mumbled to himself as he continued to look through his silver-colored protractor. "The energy is leaking out through the vortex-holes and polluting the whole place - what a palaver!" He huffed and shook his head gnomishly. "And you know what happens if anyone falls into a vortex-hole, right?"

The other two gnomes raised their eyebrows collectively and huffed together. And when gnomes huff together, you know it's not a good thing. Huffing gnomes is such a sad sight to see. After all, they work so hard to keep everything together, and rarely are they rewarded for it.

Huffing over, and within the space of a few minutes, Baga and Fender had made between them three other different piles of stones at designated spots at the back of the graveyard. During this time Mundus, in his calm and dignified way, had been strutting from one pile of stones to the next, measuring with his instrument the line of angle between each pile.

"Are you sure the *matrignome* has measured right?" Baga wiped the sweat from his brow. Fender, standing next to Baga, was sweating like he had run the gnome-marathon (which he certainly had not!).

"Right is right," said Mundus flatly. "The grid is now aligned, so time to deal with the vortex before a silly big fellow goes and falls down it." At this last comment Fender started to snigger. Mundus looked at him and half a laugh-line jiggled upon his brow. "Something amusing, my Fender Tart?" he asked.

"I was just trying to imagine a big fellow falling into a vortex," sniggered Fender.

"And?"

"And…and," wheezed Fender excitedly, "what if they woke up in the middle of a spewd of goblins, or somewhere in Tam Tower!?" Fender placed his hand over his mouth – whether in shock or laughter no one could be sure – and he stamped his feet.

"Now, gnomie, less talk of those goblins," said Mundus with a serious gnome-frown. "Their slimy, prickly ears just might get itchy and then they'll want to do something nasty. Best we don't give them something to think about. They're problem enough when they're bored. Now, it's time for patching up the vortex with a *hurdy-gurdy* song."

A few pigeons perched high upon the church steeple opened their sleepy eyes to peer down to where the three gnomes stood around a circle of stones on the ground. It would seem such an odd sight to anyone not used to the ways and wherefores of the gnome world. And no doubt, the pigeons too could hear the eerie moan coming from the ground. It sounded like the wail of a banshee as they forewarn the coming of trouble. The three gnomes formed a circle around the hole and held hands. Slowly, they began to turn anti-clockwise around the hole, and a faint hum could be heard. The hum got louder as the gnome-circle turned faster. Faster and faster the three gnomes turned, as the dance whirled with a rising chant.

Hurdy-gurdy,
gnome and sturdy,
energy weaving,
template cleaning:
fix the blockage,
unbreak the broken.

Hurdy-gurdy,
gnome and sturdy,
close this vortex,
steady the matrix:
align our realms,
balance our worlds.

Over and over again, Mundus, Baga, and Fender chanted the famous gnome *hurdy-gurdy* working song that for gnome-millennia had been used for maintaining the energy alignment of the Three Realms. After all, the Three Realms needed to be in balance for they all shared the same Earth. It was quite a spectacle, three figures in colored pointy hats whirling in a blur against the darkened night of an eerie graveyard. And they were not alone. Another pair of eyes was peering through the blackness, curious and hungry.

Soon Mundus, Baga, and Fender – all fifteen inches of them – were scrambling through the unkempt undergrowth, over bits of twigs, branches, and mossy rocks. Mundus was leading the way. They had a garden to find – and a fellow gnome to rescue. Mundus, pulling out what looked to be a pair of rubber goggles from his tool belt, surveyed the horizon.

"What do the infra-energy gnome specs say?" asked Baga in a hushed voice.

"I'm receiving an image now," replied Mundus as he scratched his chin. Fender stood behind the both of them, inspecting the little bit of dirt he had on his felt boots.

"Destination stone-gnome over that fence there!" Mundus waved for his two comrades to follow him. They scuttled up and over the fence in a dash, showing just what excellent climbers and hurdlers gnomes can be. Crouching in the grass they scanned the patch of garden before them. They were in a big fellow's garden, in the dead of Third Realm night, and they had a mission to complete. No time for fluffing it up now. Gnome-efficiency – not to mention dignity – was at stake. With Mundus leading the way, the three of them moved stealthily across the garden, up some stone steps, and onto a back patio where they saw the double doors of the conservatory. Then they froze. Mundus's jaw dropped open like a JCB digger, and he slapped his hand to his forehead. "Heeper Jeepers!" he cried out loud.

"What the gnome is wrong?" queried Baga. All three gnomes turned to look in the direction of Mundus's gaze. It was then that they saw it – their fellow stone-gnome…with a pink beard.

"Those big fellows have gone and painted poor Rundy's beard pink!" exclaimed Mundus.

"The horror, the horror!" moaned Baga.

"Pink!" squealed Fender. "But they'll never be able to de-pink it, that's what the **GRALE** manual says."

"That's right, Fender," replied Mundus softly. "Once a stone-gnome is painted, then it stays for life."

"Poor Rundy," sighed Baga, clearly overwhelmed.

At that moment a shriek rang out behind them. Only it wasn't really a shriek but more like a wailing *meowwww* as a large ginger tom cat sprang out from the shadows. Gnomes are not known for their sloth, or hesitancy. To be truthful, gnomes are more quick-witted than they are often given credit for. Mundus didn't have to yell "RUN" at the top of his gnome-voice, yet he did so all the same. Perhaps it was for dramatic effect, or out of kingly responsibility. We shall never know! What we do know is that cats like to hunt, and small fifteen-inch creatures on two legs is as good as anything – and all gnomes who venture into the Third Realm know this (see **GRALE** manual). Without hesitating further, Mundus, Baga, and Fender grabbed stone-gnome Rundy and scarpered across the grass and back to the fence from where they came. And they ran fast – as fast as fairies on amber-juice. Their behinds whooshed over the fence as if they were running the 100-meter hurdle race, with the hungry tomcat following the chase. Baga and Fender were carrying Rundy between them whilst Mundus was behind doing a strange zigzagging motion as if this was meant to confuse their feline predator. "Make for the graveyard!" shouted Mundus. "I'll meet you there." Then suddenly Mundus halted and spun around to stand his ground. The King of Grundusland was having none of this nonsense. He pulled out something from his tool belt and shook it in the air. A long baton appeared in his hands, looking like some kind of truncheon. "Come here, you snidey little ginger, and let me whack your furry little hide." The cat pounced when it was a meter away from Mundus, its claws extended with talons ready to rip him apart. Mundus spun the truncheon around his head so fast he looked like some miniature helicopter. As soon as the cat landed on the spinning whatchamacallit it was catapulted off as if it had received an electric shock. Well, we can be sure it received some kind of shock. Yelping with a sad *meuurowwee* the cat rolled across the grass and came to a final sprawl. It looked up at Mundus with cowered eyes. "That'll teach yer to mess with the bestest," shouted Mundus with a puffed-up chest. "I've fought a snotgurgle and survived – you ain't nothing for Mundus, the King of Grundusland!" And with that Mundus stuck out his tongue and blew a great unkingly *blppzzed* that sounded like a devil-imp's wind instrument. Then he ran to join the others.

"That was a close one!" wheezed Fender.

"I bet you nearly wet yourself, you smecker," teased Baga.

"Come on, you gnome-heads," said Mundus. "We need to return to the Second Realm with our poor old Rundy."

"Pink bearded Rundy," said Baga with a loud sigh.

"I guess they'll call him *pinky-beard* from now on," said Fender with a gnomish twinkle in his eye.

"Only if you start this nonsense," replied Mundus as he waved of his hand for attention. "Okay, it's time for the holy oath of a gnome." (See **HOG** - appendix). Baga and Fender squeezed their eyes shut tight and mumbled something under their breath. Soon the darkened night air around them appeared to quiver and vibrate, then go all fuzzy-like. The small gnomish bodies of Baga and Fender evaporated into the air without a sound. As soon as Mundus was sure his friends were safe, he too mumbled the secret holy oath of the gnome and melded into the vibrating air…until there was nothing, nor nobody, there.

CHAPTER TWO
AN IGNOBLE PLAN

The stone walls of the dark room were damp and dripping in fetid slime. A moldy smell lingered in the air that would make any normal person, or creature, feel faint. Yet this was no place for normal persons, or the faint-hearted – perhaps not a place for any*thing* even partly 'normal.' But the goblins that lived in Tam Tower, under the rule of the infamous Farnuk Tam, were no ordinary or *normal* goblins. They were the most irksome, troublesome, infuriating, annoying, and downright bothersome of all breeds – of all spewds – of goblins. In short, they were slimy good-for-nothings only on the lookout for making a nuisance of themselves – which they did quite frequently.

In the dim light of the room several scaly creatures were huddled on the floor picking at some scattered scraps.

"No, gimme, 'tis mine, I had my claw on it first," grunted one of the goblins.

"Git off," screeched another as it slapped the first one across its ear. The two goblins then jumped at each other and proceeded to roll across the floor, tugging at their already elongated ears and trying to snap at the other one's nose. Meanwhile, several other goblins had scurried over to the center of the room and started grabbing the bits of rotten food on the floor and stuffing it into their ugly wide mouths. The scene looked like mayhem – or just another day amongst the goblins of Tam Tower.

The room was one of many rooms that spiraled up, floor after floor, of the great tower that Urnuk Tam, father of Vernuk Tam and grandfather of Farnuk Tam, had built. These were the scaly descendants of the legendary Kaufuk Tam, greatest defiler in beastly goblin history. Or so the story is told. If truth be told (and there is little truth where goblins are concerned), nobody really knows if the 'legendary' Kaufuk Tam ever existed. It's really a question of no goblin daring to question the story or having the brains to even think about it. But that is all beside the point, as the current 'goblin-in-charge' was Farnuk Tam, and Tam Tower was now his – and this was undisputed. No one messed with the Tam family, not amongst the goblins anyway. The Tams were the Tams, the heirs of Tam Tower, and that was that. Anything else was just goblin-snot, gnome-fluff, or fairy-rumor as far as any half-decent goblin was concerned.

A goblin with a particularly wrinkled, weaselly face was wringing his hands together and nodding his head. "Yes, your audacious one, I shall call them together. It shall be done, on time."

"Immediately, you cretin!" came a harsh, grating voice from above the cowered goblin. "Not *on time,* you smelly non-grammatical goblin – it's *immediately*! Didn't your putrid goblin brood never teach you anything?" Farnuk Tam was shouting down to his deputy, Wenkle Frat.

Wenkle, weaselly and wrinkled, was nodding his scaly goggle-eyed goblin head frantically. "Yes, my mighty audacious one, you are so beastly right as always. Immediately I shall go and get the others." And saying that, Wenkle scuttled off like a slithering lizard on skates.

Farnuk sat several feet above, perched upon a slime-covered stone throne. His goblin feet were dangling over the edge of the throne, unable to touch the floor, and his bony green-grey fingers were tapping on its sides. Farnuk, like all the goblins of the Second Realm, was of a predominantly scaly green shade, with greasy skin. Goblins walk about, very ably, on flat feet; and their bulging eyeballs have lizard-like slits, with a hint of yellowy-orange. There is also something toad-like about them, combined with their big pointy ears that also gives them a bat-ness look. All in all, goblins are seemingly a mixture of lizard, toad, and bat; and stand (in human Third Realm terms) about 20 inches tall – just a wee bit taller than gnomes. Farnuk, however, like all the Tams before him, had a greyer tinge to his skin. Farnuk was sure that this grey tone made him look meaner and more goblin-fierce than all the rest. It was a mark of the greatness of the Tam goblin brood; he was sure about that. There wasn't a single goblin doubt in his devious little head. Furthermore, Farnuk knew that it was up to him to devise the next daring and brutal plan against those soppy, fairy-loving, hippy-like gnomes that were always spoiling things. Of this, Farnuk was doubly, triply, goblinly sure! That was why Farnuk had called this meeting together. Things were about to change. That is, things were about to get devious. Farnuk grinned to himself. He loved grinning to himself. It made him feel even more devious than he was doubly sure he already was.

A spewd of goblins had gathered in the throne room and were mulling about restlessly beneath the grand stone throne where Farnuk was sitting. Wenkle called them all to order. Well, into the best sort of order possible between greasy goblins. Farnuk cleared his throat and all the goblins finally stopped squabbling amongst themselves and stood to attention. Their boggly, green goblin eyes were all focused upon Farnuk Tam, their most devious leader.

"It's time for action," growled Farnuk, raising his skinny fist into the air. "Our little raiding parties in this realm are not enough. Chaos in the Second Realm is getting boring. We need to expand!" All the goblins cheered and spluttered in agreement with Farnuk's words, even if they had little idea of what he was getting at. "We need to move on up!" continued Farnuk, as all the goblins raised their stupid heads to the ceiling as if something was really 'up' there. He shook his head with a sigh. "You cretinous imp-pushers! No, we need to go up, up, up…more badder and meaner than before. We need to get back into the Third Realm and start messing about with those humans. Why should those gnomes get all the Third Realm fun, eh?!"

"Because we were thrown out of Third Realm?" replied a young voice somewhere in the goblin spewd.

Farnuk immediately jumped to his feet. "Rhetorical, it was a rhetorical question, you globulous imp-head," he snapped at the top of his voice. All the goblins looked at each other with blank faces and shrugged. All except Wenkle that is, who was grunting and nodding his head in praiseworthy approval of Farnuk's words. "I have a plan!" Farnuk sneered about the room and sat down. "We are going to kidnap the gnome guard of the Blue Portal, and then pass through the Blue Portal into the Third Realm. Now, isn't that simple?" There was silence. "No, that's not a rhetorical question. You can answer!" He sighed and shook his head.

"Simple, yess," said a rather scaly and scar-faced goblin with more than normal bulging eyes. It was Peasly Greel, the senior goblin officer and captain of the goblin army. "It isss simple but not also. Once we are in the Third Realm we cannot return without the Portal Password. What those damn gnomies call the **HOG**. We all knows zhat, sire."

"Indeed we do, Peasly – which is why I have thought beyond that. My plan is that we not only kidnap the gnome guard but we get him to reveal his holy oath of a gnome. Once we know this oath we can cross, re-cross, and return from here to there whenever we like. And we'll create chaos for those humans and gnomes alike!"

"That's a mighty ignacious plan, o daring one," sniggered Wenkle in his usual slimy way.

"It's *audacious* – you illiterate nose-picker!" Farnuk rolled his eyes and gurgled. Wenkle cowered his eyes and gave Farnuk a pleading look. "It's not only audacious, but also downright brilliantly *ignoble*." Farnuk stopped as if to think. Then he grinned to himself. "Yeah, I like that name," he said with a self-satisfactory nod. "That's what I'm going to call it – my Ignoble Plan! And I also have an Ignoble Plan B, of course." Farnuk eyed the goblins in the room as silence fell over them like slime-snot. He stood up to make full effect for his next words. "What is the gnomes' greatest weakness?" he called out with great fanfare to the room. Still silence. "Well? Speak up, you imp-pushers – or have you got gnome fluff on your tongues?"

"Their beards?" asked one of the goblins.

"Their brains!" shouted out another, to which the whole spewd fell into a guffaw of squealing goblin laughter.

"You stinky-fingers!" roared Farnuk. "It's you who don't have the brains. You're all a bunch of fairy-dreamers. These gnomes have brains – and beards – and they have strong legs that help them run faster than bog urchins. But their greatest weakness is human eyes – aha!" Still further stunned silence. You could hear a goblin-skinflake drop.

"Human eyes?" said Peasly, finally.

"Yes, human eyes, you slimy fools. Whenever humans set eyes on gnomes they turn to stone. All we have to do is get ourselves a load of human eyes, and then we go marching into Grundusland and turn every one of those fairy-loving gnomes to stone. Grundusland will be ours!"

"That's beastly brilliiaant!" snorted Wenkle and wrung his greasy hands together.

"Indeed, it is. I, the bold and mightily Farnuk Tam, will go down in goblin-story as the greatest goblin since the legendary dastardly Kaufuk Tam. Peasly, gather a few of your best grimy goblins and get me a gnome guard from the Blue Portal."

"Yesss, sire," hissed Peasly, and saluted. All the other goblins in the room cheered – or rather growled, grunted, and gurgled – in agreement. The goblin spewd in Tam Tower were getting feisty and ready for some deviance.

Over at Octagon Lodge…Baga and Fender materialized first through the Blue Portal, carrying between them the stoned figure of Rundy, complete with a pink-colored beard. A few seconds later Mundus appeared through the quivering Blue Portal.

"Damn pesky furrballs," he muttered. Baga and Fender were standing a few feet away, brushing off the dust from their stone comrade. The three gnomes were standing in the Octagon Lodge that housed the Blue Portal. It was a sacred and special place that was under the guard and protection of the gnomes. Or rather, to be more precise, it was under the custodianship of the King of Grundusland, which at this time happened to be Mundus Grundy (son of Burgus Grundy). And since gnomes live a very long time, both Mundus's parents – Burgus and Merly – were still alive and well and living in the top turret of Grundy Castle. They had long ago decided to leave the running of Grundusland to

Mundus, so they could enjoy their final centuries in peace and quiet.

"Nature is getting a little cranky out in Third Realm, hey Mundus," said Baga, still a little breathless from the run.

"Mmmm. Not only Nature, but the whole energy of the Third Realm is slipping out of place. Those big fellows are sure messing it up," replied Mundus. He was looking concerned.

Baga leaned in close until their wrinkled gnomish faces were only a few inches away from each other. "I think this means we have to step up our work in the Third Realm. We have our gnomish duty to maintain the energy grid – it's part of our *contract*. We'll have to risk more visits."

Mundus nodded in agreement, then pointed to Fender and the stoned Rundy. "You better get going to gnome de-stoning if we ever wish to see Rundy with us again. And for pity's sake, don't let him look into a mirror!"

Outside the Octagon Lodge the two gnome brothers Lompa and Jompa were standing guard and, as always, arguing between themselves over the most boring things.

"A river blockage in the Third Realm is more important than a fallen tree," said Lompa, his voice sounding as lively as a plank of wood.

"'Tis not," replied Jompa with a little huff. "A fallen tree is so dangerous that you can hit your head on it."

"Then you should watch where you're going. But a blocked river stops the energy from flowing. Now that is more important – and I know I'm right, bro'," said Lompa in his deadpan way.

"You're about as right as a backward-headed gurglefish going in the wrong direction. That's how right you not be, you block-head," snapped Jompa.

"Stop bickering, you pair of huffalots." Mundus let out a belly-chuckle as he walked up behind the two gnome brothers. "I can hear your rumblings from inside the lodge, you gnome-heads! Now you know we only need one gnome on guard, so Jompa you come with me and leave Lompa to guard in peace."

Jompa and Lompa saluted each other with a grimace and a wrinkled-up nose. Then Jompa turned and followed Mundus over the track to Grundy City – the heart of Grundusland. The city was not very far away. In fact, nothing was far away in Grundusland; that way the gnomes managed to keep everything neat and organized. Grundusland was surrounded by a large forest, as gnomes love nothing better than being beside Nature. And when the Second Realm was matter-realized into existence (known as the *Big Vibration*), the gnomes were provided with their Nature-filled land, full of countless varieties of trees, shrubs, and plants. For if there is one thing that gnomes do well it is looking after Nature. Of course, they have the sprites and devas to help them too.

Grundy City lay in the heart of the forest where there was a large clearing. And the pinnacle of this gnome city-state was the large stone Grundy Castle, with turrets higher than the highest trees. From the highest tower one could see, on a clear day, the dark outline of Tam Tower festering in the distance. The goblins, after their shenanigans in the Third Realm, were banished to the Second Realm and told to keep well clear of the gnomes and their important work. But you know goblins, they just can't keep out of trouble…not even if their slimy lives depended on it.

That's why, at the farthest edge of the forest, a small motley band of goblins were sneaking their way through the trees ready to kidnap a gnome. The leading goblin, Peasly Greel, was hopping ahead like a demented spring chicken while his three lieutenants followed behind as best they could. Peasly had a large coil of rope hung over his shoulder and one of the lieutenants had a big sack under his arm. Their bulging eyes and intense grimaces showed to all who could see that they meant business. Soon, Peasly and his mini squadron of elite goblin soldiers reached the border of the clearing. Not far away, set back and isolated from Grundy City, was the Octagon Lodge. And inside the lodge, as everyone knew, was the Blue Portal.

"Now what's the plan, boss?" asked the goblin with the big sack.

"Zhiss is zhe plan," replied Peasly, before pausing. He scratched his long ear and in a quick burst spurted out – "Grab the gnome, sack him and scarper!" All four goblins looked at each other blankly, as if their shared brain cell was figuring out how to interpret that last message. Then Peasly started running and hopping madly as if he'd ingested a mouthful of yucky fairy dust. The three goblin lieutenants began to scurry after him with their bat-like scaly ears flopping in the back draft. Poor old Lompa didn't really know what was happening before the four hopping goblins were on top of him. To be fair, he didn't have much time to see what was going on as he was gazing in the opposite direction at the river and gnome-daydreaming about building a dam. The next thing he knew there were several goblins jumping on his back and a lot of gargling and spluttering around him. Lompa was thrust to the floor and a rope tied around him several times. He was then picked up from the floor and bungled into a sack. That's when the girlish giggling started.

"Got us a gnome, boss…heeweeeheee," sniggered one of the lieutenant gnomes.

"We're gonna jump up and down on him, we are, and then smother him with imp-goo…eeerrrargghhh."

"Stop it, you gob-heads, we gozza get back shuper-sharpish," commanded Peasly. "Now you zhree carry him and let's get out of here." The gaggle of goblins darted back the way they had come and disappeared into the forest, carrying with them the sack with Lompa wriggling inside. Of course, the goblins forgot to put something over Lompa's mouth to stop him shouting; and Lompa did shout – all the way through the forest.

"I'll box your ugly goblin ears in when I get outta this sack – you miserable rubber-headed bat-for-brains!" roared Lompa. "When the gnomes get hold of you wretched bunch, they will dunk you all in a river of slime-snot for a week. You're all slobber-bellied good-for-nothings!" Et cetera, et cetera, et cetera. Well, you get the picture. You shouldn't really tie-up a gnome. Gnomes are freedom loving little people, who just hate – really hate – being constrained. And Lompa would have been even angrier had he known where the goblins were taking him.

CHAPTER THREE
CAPTIVITY (OR GNOME ALONE)

Somewhere, in a dark room in Tam Tower…it looked like a small shady figure was squatting on the ground, gesturing wildly in the air as if a mad demented bogey. The room was dank, the air stuffy and musty, and only a very low light illuminated the scene. The little figure seemed to be whispering, as if in conversation with someone else. Yet this was no bogey, no brownie, no kobold, nor gremlin – it was an imp. A little mischievous imp called Bodel Nak who was well known among the goblins, if little understood. It was said that Bodel was a helper of the goblins; yet this little imp generally kept himself private. Or, as some suspected, he preferred to be alone so he could plot his roguish scams. And this time Bodel the imp was trying his impish charm on the whispery, smoky silhouette of Kluth the djinn. Whereas Bodel was a smaller, short-eared version of a goblin, with a flatter nose and less bulging eyes, Kluth was far from physical. Djinns were like shadows – they moved like whispers, often formless and invisible. They presented themselves in a smoky form when they desired; and nobody, not even Farnuk, could command their service. In the end, no one could ever be sure whether to trust a djinn or not. Djinns had their own annoying sense of free will, which they employed as they saw fit. Nobody knew when a djinn was coming, going, or in the middle of coming-and-going.

"It's our time I tell you!" implored Bodel in a low hushed whisper. "Those goblins couldn't organize a snot contest in the middle of a slime field. They're all fairy-dreamers with gnome-fluff in their brains. But you and I know better. We could really run the show around here. You know it's true, Kluth – you're the man, the dude!"

"Yesss," replied a low voice. The voice of Kluth sounded like a dull, disinterested echo that stuck to the dank walls. It was a voice that could send a shiver up your spine and make your ears feel damp. "That may be so," continued the voice of the semi-visible djinn. "Yet why not let the goblins get on with things. Why take the trouble ourselves?"

"Power!" urged Bodel, almost jumping up and down. "We'll have the power to run this place. Maybe then we could take over Grundusland and have the whole realm for ourselves, yeah? What do you say, old pal?"

"Well," replied Kluth slowly…ever so slowly, seemingly apathetic. "We could, we could…yet there is a better way."

"Yes, yes, tell me, tell me," insisted Bodel excitedly.

"Well, we could let the goblins get on with their plan to defeat the gnomes, and *then* make our move to take control. That way we won't have to worry about the gnomes as the goblins will have already taken care of them. You see, one less bother for us."

"Eek, it's briiiliant!" squeaked Bodel, who was now stamping his little impish foot with delight.

"Ssshh, you crazy little imp," implored Kluth. "You will attract Her!"

"Who?" asked Bodel

"The fiendish one," hissed Kluth. The shadow that was Kluth then seemed to shiver, or rather go fuzzy at the edges, as a larger shadow loomed up from behind.

"WHAT'S going on here?" boomed a voice that bounced off the walls like fatty echoes. Bodel sank even smaller into his body and his head shriveled to the size of a bogey egg. Kluth gave off a sound something like a gulp.

"Errr…nothing, my dearest one – just chatting with friends."

In another dark room in Tam Tower…Lompa, a strong yet unadventurous gnome of a respectable 295 gnome years, found himself in the not so respectable position of being tied to a wooden rack. Around him were several goblins grinning stupidly from ear to big ear, and their pointy little teeth showing all the bits of food still stuck between them.

"Let's poke him," said one of the goblins.

"Nah, that's no fun. We should cut his beard off and stuff it in his silly gnomish hat!" said another, to which the rest squealed in laughter.

"Touch me," growled Lompa, "and my brother will come to box your brains into marsh mash and feed it to the swamp eels."

"Ohh, he's a tough one," sniggered the first goblin.

"We gnomes have a duty, a contract, and we are needed. But what do you lot do, eh? You just squeal, snigger, snort, and make darn trouble!" Lompa tried to struggle out of his fastenings, yet he was firmly tied down.

"Oh, but we're here to make you squirm…jejejejeje!" Suddenly, the sniggering stopped as the goblins turned around to see Farnuk approach with his deputy, Wenkle.

"We are here to create some chaos, of course," said Farnuk with a sneer. "Chaos is a necessary thing – just as necessary as you boring, orderly gnomes. You need us, just as all the realms need us." Farnuk puffed out his chest, obviously proud of himself.

"Bahh," grunted Lompa. "We gnomes don't need you. You goblins just mess things up, as always!"

"Mmm…I'm not so sure you're really getting this. Look, the world needs a little disruption. This is the goblin way. We are here because you are here, and you are here because of us. We keep things in balance – dastardly is the new cool!" Farnuk sniggered and elbowed Wenkle in his scaly side. Lompa just stayed where he was, with a big frown upon his furrowed face (well, he wasn't exactly going anywhere since he was tied down to a rack). It was clear that Lompa was not having any of this and was not the least impressed with Farnuk's explanations. And from the blank faces of the other goblins, it was clear they hadn't understood any of Farnuk's words either. "Well, my little bearded dude, we goblins need to get into the Third Realm and so we need your holy oath. So, just give it to us and that's that – no more fairy-fluffing around," Farnuk said and tried to make a slimy goblin wink at Lompa. Lompa's face went whiter than a yeti's scalp.

"My **HOG**? The Holy Oath of a Gnome? Never! I'd rather eat ogre droppings!" Lompa huffed defiantly.

Farnuk smiled. "Well, that can always be arranged. Have it your way. You are going to have to tell us whether you lump it or loathe it. We goblins have ways of making you talk. Don't you worry your little gnomie belly about that." And then Farnuk gave a hard poke of his spiny finger into Lompa's stomach.

"Ouch!"

A little later, in yet another dark room at the top of Tam Tower…Farnuk was sitting on his stone throne with a brooding look on his scaly goblin face. Just below him stood his deputy, Wenkle Frat, and his Chief Officer, Peasly Greel; both were looking slightly nervous.

"Well?" snapped Farnuk.

"Well, what?" replied Wenkle after a little uncomfortable silence.

"Do we have ways of making that damn gnome talk? We need that **HOG** – no holy oath, no Ignoble plan!" Farnuk looked at his two most senior henchmen, yet neither of them looked confident.

"We could tickle him until he confesses," suggested Wenkle.

"Sniper-dipers! That's no dastardly good. Gnomes are as ticklish as stone gargoyles on a sleeping holiday," rasped Farnuk.

"We could cut out his thongue to make him thalk," lisped a peevish Peasly.

"Oh, good one, Peasly – you stinky-finger! Yeah, let's cut out his tongue. What a brilliant idea, no wonder I made you my chief officer. You've got less goblin brain cells than a headless troll, you gnome-fluff!" Farnuk slapped Peasly over his head with one his dangly legs. "Come on, come on, you festering warts, we need a plan. We need to get that gnome to talk. Dah, and double slime-snot!"

"Oh, supremely badacious one, your goblin cleverness, why don't we kidnap the gnomes's wife and blackmail him?" said Wenkle, wringing his hands in obvious delight.

"And what if he doesn't have a wife?" replied Farnuk, raising his scaly eyebrow.

"The the thhen we only pretend to kidnap her," suggested Peasly with a smirk. Whack! "Ouuchh!"

"Does no one have a plan here?" roared Farnuk in a mighty goblin squeal. "Am I surrounded by brainless bograts!" An uncomfortable slimy silence followed, until broken by…

"Why, great Farnuk Tam, of course you have a plan."

The sound of a slithery voice attracted Farnuk's attention. It was the imp Bodel Nak. Farnuk screwed his eyes together as he watched the little imp come closer. Bodel had proved useful in the past, as imps and goblins had often worked together in their devilish schemes. Yet Bodel was an elusive imp, just turning up when he wanted – or at just the right time?

Somewhere in the other dark room in Tam Tower…poor old (or rather not so old) Lompa was being interrogated by two of Peasly's officers. They had removed Lompa's boots and with their tickling stick (made from swamp weed) they had been trying for the past half hour to get Lompa to laugh. Yet they couldn't even manage to get the slightest smirk out of him. Exasperated they had given up and moved on to their next plan: to use itching nukk bugs. These tiny little bugs would nip at the skin causing an almighty itching until the urge to scratch becomes irresistible. And so nukk bugs were placed over Lompa's bare arms as he lay helplessly strapped to the rack. Lompa's strained face showed that he was trying all he could to resist the incredible need to scratch himself. So Lompa did what all gnomes do under extreme stress – they start to grind their teeth. Oh, and gnomes have double sets of extra-large, extra strong molars on each side of the mouth that are like industrial crunchers. That's because, at one time, gnomes used to chomp and chew their way through hard soil and rock when they worked in the mines. But that was another age ago, before gnomes settled down to a pastoral existence. And it just so happened that this gnome wasn't called 'Lompa the Chomper' for nothing…

Grrrzzzzzqrrrzzrrrr…Lompa began grinding his huge molars together as if crushing pebbles into fine powder. The infuriating noise kept on getting louder and LOUDER – chomping, grinding, scraping, scrapping, trawling, screeching, pulverizing…GREEZZZZZZQRRRZZZRRR…a sound like scratching a thousand fingernails across endless chalkboards.

"Ahh! Stop that infernal noise," screamed one of the goblin interrogators.

"Erghhh, it's driving me crazy, cut it out, you damn gnome," screeched the other goblin, as he hopped around madly with his hands clasped over this pointy ears. Yet the noise went on…grinding, growling, churning, grating, clenching, crushing, gnashing, mincing, munching…

"It's 'ORIBBLE!"

"It's gnome-awful!"

"It's fairy-dreadful!" The goblins shouted and squealed as they ran around the room in despair, clasping their eyes, then their ears, and hopping up and down madly. Things, it seemed, were getting nowhere. Then again, what could one expect from goblin interrogation? Sometimes you have to ask the right questions in order to get the answers you need. Other times it may not be a question of asking anything at all. There are ways, and then there are other ways.

"Our ways," said Bodel, "must be more subtle. Interrogation is just so primitive. It's just so, well, so human. Goblins must have a little more tact."

"Tact? What do you mean by tact, you little imp?" said Farnuk, squinting at Bodel Nak who was squatting before the stone throne.

"Tact is more indirect. Rather than bashing down the front door we should be going around to the back door," continued Bodel with a roll of his eyes. He obviously loved his time to play the advisor.

"Front door, back door, tact, toe, tum – talk sense to me, you infernal little imp before I have your knees sown together!" Farnuk was spluttering impatiently. A coy impish smile erupted over the face of Bodel Nak.

"Why, of course. What I am saying is that you are not going to get the Holy Oath of a Gnome by simple interrogation. The gnomes cannot give away their **HOG**. They simply cannot because it is conditioned into them from birth. It is a part of them. So, the way to get it from them is to de-condition them." Bodel smiled. Farnuk pursed his green-grey goblin lips and was obviously thinking.

"And how do we – or rather how do I – de-condition this annoying gnome?'

Bodel waved his impish little hand. "Well, you hypnotize him, of course. Forget the personality, go directly to the inner part of the gnome where all the secrets are kept. Once you are inside him, he won't be able to stop you getting what you want. And what's even better is that he won't know that he's told you; which means you can release him and the other gnomes won't know a thing. Your secret is safe, and as far as the other gnomes are concerned their holy oath is also safe." Bodel cocked his head confidently to one side and grinned at Farnuk.

"Yess, this is audacious indeed," Farnuk said with a smirk.

"Yess," echoed Bodel, "it really is an Ignoble plan."

"But who will do the hypnotizing? This is not a goblin skill," said Farnuk suddenly, realizing this could be a problem.

"No problem," replied Bodel smugly. "I have just the guy you need."

"I will stop," growled Lompa through gritted teeth, "when you get these blasted biting bugs offa me."

"Take 'em orf, take 'em orf," yelled one of the goblins from the far side of the room. The other goblin, who was nearer, ran to snatch off all the nukk bugs that were crawling over Lompa's arms. The molar grinding and crunching finally stopped and the goblins collapsed exhausted on the floor.

"You really are silly goblins. I bet you wouldn't know the first thing about patching up dams or de-blocking rivers," said Lompa with a shake of his head.

"That's because us goblins don't get much chance to hop around in the Third Realm," said Farnuk as he strolled into the darkened room where Lompa was tied up. "Mmm, this guest room really is a bit bare. Remind me to ask Peasly to put some more snot on the walls."

"You're getting nothing from me," protested Lompa.

"Ah, don't worry, dear gnomie chappie. We goblins don't want anything from you. It's all been a terrible misunderstanding. I do ap-ol-o-gize, Mr. Gnomey Whomey," said Farnuk in a ridiculously false caring voice. "I told my officers to find me a small bone, not a small 'gnome.' Well, mistakes happen." Farnuk shrugged and smirked at the same time.

"That's all well and good," huffed Lompa. "Now get me down from here before I invoke the Shining Ones."

Farnuk grimaced. He always got a funny feeling in the gut of his goblin belly whenever anyone mentioned the Shining Ones. The memory of those who banished the goblins to the dark corner of Second Realm all those epochs ago still lingered in goblin cells. Their name was still invoked as a curse or a blessing. A shiver ran down Farnuk's scaly spine.

"Well, before we let you go, we need to read you your rights as a free gnome within Tam Tower. It's all part of our new democratic policies," said Farnuk. At that moment a large cloud of dense smoke entered the room and began to approach. The brownish smoke closely resembled the outline of a tall figure, yet no features could be seen. Lompa strained his eyes and tried to make out this strange apparition.

"This is Kluth, our resident rights lawyer," said Farnuk with a little shrug. "Just look at him closely while he reads you your rights." Kluth moved towards Lompa until he was almost over him.

"Look into me and follow my words," said an eerie, shadowy voice. Farnuk, and everybody else, slowly stepped back and crept away.

Back in the dark room at the top of Tam Tower... Farnuk was giggling in his chair, feeling well pleased with himself as Bodel Nak walked in.

"Well, well, do we have the **HOG** or not?" Farnuk asked excitedly. A large impish grin crept over Bodel's pimpled face as his eyes light up.

"Indeed, we do, sire," said Bodel with a broad sneer as he walked up to Farnuk. Farnuk bent down to let Bodel whisper in his ear. Farnuk too then joined Bodel in grinning inanely. Wenkle and Peasly were standing a few feet away in great anticipation. Wenkle, as usual, was wringing his hands together, yet still a little angry that Bodel should steal Farnuk's favor from him. And Peasly was thinking about getting his squadron together to go on a Third Realm raiding party – now, that would be something to tell the goblin-boys!

"Peasly, bring your Elite Goblin Squadron here!" ordered Farnuk.

"Yesss, sir!" saluted Peasly before dashing off.

"And you, Wenkle, bring that branding machine here. Y'know, the old one that we used to use for writing silly names on goblin thieves."

"Sire, oh badacious one, are we getting branded with silly names?" asked Wenkle with a worried look.

"Not quite," replied Farnuk with a wicked smile. "We're all getting a new tattoo."

CHAPTER FOUR
THE EARTH SHAKES

Mundus Grundy, King of all Grundusland, was bending over his herb garden planting some new hot and spicy plants when the news came in that Lompa had been kidnapped and released. Lompa had arrived back in Grundy City a bit dazed and confused but basically fine and unharmed. It appeared that he had been mistaken for a 'small bone,' or so Lompa had said.

"A small bone?" Mundus said surprised. Baga shrugged his shoulders. Jompa, Lompa's twin brother, was standing with them in the royal gardens.

"That's what my brother says," said Jompa scratching his beard. He couldn't figure it out either and was just as dazed as his brother. Not that either of them had much imagination between them both. Mundus, however, was a little wiser, and quick-witted.

"This doesn't make a bum-fluff of sense," muttered Mundus quietly to himself, although not quietly enough.

"Sure doesn't," agreed Baga, grinning at Mundus's kingly remark.

"Whenever those rubber-bellied goblins get involved in something then it's for a bad reason. They're up to no good, I can feel it. My gnome senses tell me that those goblins have got some silly ideas in their heads."

"Do you think they're going to attack us?" asked Jompa worriedly.

Grundus shook his head. 'No, I don't think so. The goblins are not that brave – or clever. They make trouble, they mess with people, and they mess things up. They like nothing more than creating chaos. That's all they've ever done since the dawn of the **CBE** – since we agreed to the 'Contract for all **B**eings on **E**arth.' The goblins have always been the wild card, amongst other things!"

"I don't understand," said Jompa with a blank look. "What has this got to do with our work in maintaining the energy vortexes of the Third Realm?"

"Everything! Nothing lasts forever; change is the one unavoidable law. One day this too will pass," said Mundus with a sweep of his hand over Grundy City.

"Don't say that, Mundus!" Baga squirmed a little uncomfortably as he tried to imagine the end of Grundy City.

"It's true, my gnome brother. We gnomes may be ageless, and our Gnome Inheritance passed down from generation to generation. Yet the realms we live in must change, otherwise they will stagnate. My father knew this, and his father before him, and his father and forefathers and all the other Grundy fathers before him. We are custodians to ongoing change and that's our duty, gnome brothers."

"And what have the goblins got to do with this?" asked Jompa.

Mundus gave a sympathetic smile. "There are different types of change. One is smooth and gradual, and the other is more chaotic and abrupt. Sometimes we need the chaotic change, sometimes the smooth. Yet we cannot escape either. And I've suspected for a while now that something is coming." Mundus put down his trowel and grinned. "I just love showtime!"

Not too far away in the Grundusland Forest...a disorderly gaggle of goblins, calling themselves the Elite Goblin Squadron, were making their way through the undergrowth. They were trying to act like commandos, with blackened faces, and dodging behind trees as if they were goblin-invisible. At the head of the pack crept Chief Officer Peasly, also with a blacked-out commando face. Of course, goblins being goblins, all of them had forgotten to black out their bat-like ears too. The result was a bunch of blackened faces, with green pointy ears, darting, not too stealthily, from tree to tree with the occasional commando roll on the forest floor. Not quite pathetic, yet certainly not scary.

"Ssshh, quit zhat whisthling," ordered Peasly.

"But it's the goblin Gung-Ho tune," protested one of the elite squadron goblins.

"Right, get in formathon – check zhe rear," commanded Peasly. At the back of the line was the imp Bodel Nak, picking at his scrawny teeth with a little stick. Beside him loomed two large dark shapes. Both dark shapes looked like congealed smoke, with a reddish glow in the center of the dark mass.

"Kluth, is everything fine?" asked Bodel, a little suspiciously. The dark mass began to go a little fuzzy around the edges.

"YESSS..." said a low moaning voice.

"And your missus?"

"THAT'S ENOUGH, impertinent imp," bellowed a second low voice. "You address me as Konji and nothing else – got it?"

"Yep," shrugged Bodel, attempting to sound indifferent. Bodel was trying his best to act casual, yet he knew that the two djinns, Kluth and Konji, were powerful and important allies. And the only way to enlist their help was to entice them with promises of power. The agreement between the djinns and the goblins was for the djinns to hypnotize the gnome Portal guards long enough for the Goblin Elite Squadron to enter into Third Realm, steal as many human eyes as possible, then to return to the Second Realm. The djinns would then release the guards from their hypnosis, making sure they remembered nothing of what had happened. The goblins would then be armed with human eyes, be incredibly dangerous – or so they believed – and ready for Plan B of the Ignoble Plan. And the poor old gnomes would continue gardening and looking after rivers, without suspecting a thing. Farnuk was sure the whole idea was just pure slime goblin-genius. Then again, he would. Bodel Nak, on the other hand, wasn't planning on having the gnome guards hypnotized for too long. They needed to be ready for the goblins to return. And with the Elite Goblin Squadron under gnome arrest, it would leave fewer goblins to guard a vulnerable Tam Tower. Now that, thought Bodel, was even purer slime imp-genius. Yet the djinns, Kluth and Konji, were an element of uncertainty…

The squadron of goblins, including Bodel, Kluth, and Konji, arrived at the farthest East border of Grundusland. Well, it's called Grundusland but it's not exactly an empire, nor a country. It is an area of the Second Realm that is mostly green and forestry. It has hills, rivers, parks, etc., all the usual Nature stuff that gnomes just love. And they look after it with such care and dedication, almost as if in practice for their Third Realm maintenance duties. In the middle of Grundusland is a large forest with an open park area where sits Grundy City, the home to most of the gnomes (although there are still some neo-primitives who prefer to build stick shelters in the fields and live 'off the gnome-grid'). Mundus Grundy, as the current King, lived in the castle at the center of the city. There are usually no guards around the castle since all the gnomes trust each other, and it's an open gnomocracy (see **BOGGLE** in appendix). There's no tax either – but that's a whole other story. To the east, just beyond the city gates, lies the Octagon Lodge, which houses the Blue Portal. The Shining Ones warned the gnomes not to have the portal within the city just in case the blue-fusion energies exploded one day. So, there it lies, close to the forest that borders Grundusland – exactly where we find the goblin squadron at this very moment.

The goblins were all gathered together to focus on the task ahead. Well, perhaps focused is not the right word – more like they had their eyes in the same direction. Peasly ordered each goblin to check his arms. They lifted up both their arms to where they had the **HOG** tattooed so they would not forget. After all, goblins are known to forget more times than they care to remember! Etched into the left arm were the words, heart ~ soul. And on the right arm the words, love ~ service.

"Right, goblin squadron," whispered Peasly, "zhis is zhe plan. We all enter zegether into zhe Third Realm. Zwo of you come with me; we steal zhe eyes and zhe rest create your chaos. Bodil will stay here with zhe djinns and keep the Portal gnome-free. Whatever you do, don't lose your arms or you won't get back!" Then the goblins crouched in the shrubbery whilst the djinns, like dark shadows, went off to do their hypnotic work.

*****

38

It wasn't long before the Elite Goblin Squadron were jumping and hopping through the Blue Portal like deliriously frantic frogs, with their new **HOG** password. The world was now open to them – or rather, the Third Realm was. The goblins landed in a field on the outskirts of a small town. An early light was soon to creep over the horizon, signaling the sunrise of a new day in the human realm. All the goblins stood still in amazement, as if mesmerized by the light and colors of the Third Realm. Each of them had an officer's sack slung over their shoulder, filled with goblin-knows-what dastardly gadgets.

"What are the coordinates, Squad Leader?" asked one of the goblins, breaking the silence.

"Coordinates?" replied Peasly with a confused look. "Ermm, coordinates are 00.12345.00." The goblin officer remained motionless, without even a twitch on his scaly face or a blink of his eyes. In the goblin world, if you have nothing to say, and there is nothing bouncing around in the head, no thoughts or anything, the body just does nothing. It is as if there is nobody at home.

"Leave zhe zricky stuff zo me, officer," smirked Peasly. "All you need zo know is zhat we're going zo zown."

"Zo Zown?" Again, the complete immobility returned.

"Yep, zo zown. Follow me!"

The goblins, being goblins, could not know the difference between a town and a village. In fact, they were not even sure where in the Third Realm they were. As it happened, they had landed near a village within Greater London. They were, more or less (or less or more), within the heartland of the Third Realm. In the small village of Pratt's Bottom the residents were not yet awake. Or if awake, they were indoors keeping cozy and safe. Little did they suspect that a spewd of goblins had arrived on their doorstep.

First, the goblins got to work on the easy stuff – trashing gardens. In between sniggers, the members of the Elite Goblin Squadron proceeded to uproot vegetable plants, stomp all over newly prepared seed beds, rip down growing vines, over-turn plant pots, and move the garden furniture. Just really, really making a mess of every garden they could get their grubby goblin hands on. The sniggering, tittering, snorting, gurgling, babbling, and goblin burbling filled the air. Luckily for the goblins it was all below the hearing range of the humans inside their houses. Goblins like to make a riot, but they certainly don't want to explain themselves to humans. Meanwhile, Peasly and two of his officers went searching for a hospital, the place most likely to have a ready store of human eyes. Farnuk had told Peasly not to return empty handed. And if he couldn't find any eyes then he would have to extract them directly from humans. If that was the case, thought Peasly's two brain cells, then sick humans in hospital would put up less of a fight. A hospital, it seemed, was the perfect place.

"Find me a hospital, and quickly," hissed Peasly.

"Eye, eye!" said both officers, before bursting into fits of giggles.

"Zhis is no zhime for goblin giggles," retorted Peasly angrily, and stormed off. Other members of the Elite Goblin Squadron had now broken into sheds and were throwing the contents out onto lawns. Others were trying to block fountains by sticking objects into the jet nozzle. Some more adventurous ones were messing with the road signs – twisting them around to face the other way or bending them so drivers could no longer see the instructions. This goblin squadron came prepared for Third Realm chaos.

One or two of the goblins had taken out large tubes of goo-glue from their packs and were running down the main street gluing up the letterboxes of each shop. Another goblin had a spray can and was working on some goblin graffiti which, to be honest, was not a work of art. Others were busy stuffing the exhaust pipes of parked cars with whatever they could find in the rubbish bins. All in all, things were going crazy in Pratt's Bottom. But it was not only the physical things which the goblins were messing with. The fact that they were in the Third Realm was itself a problem, as the local energy matrix was not used to unauthorized Second Realm invasions. The 'energy signature' of the goblins is very different from that of the gnomes. Whereas the gnomes are in balance with the Third Realm matrix, the goblins are very definitely not. Too many goblins in the Third Realm for too long a time, and the Earth may start to shake…literally. Farnuk and his spewd of goblins were not aware of this, and even if they did know they probably wouldn't care. After all, what greater chaos is there than a shaking Earth?

Back in Grundy City…Mundus was stretching out on his deckchair at the back porch of the castle. His boots were on the floor, and Mundus was inspecting his hairy, thickset feet.

"What you be doing now, you little Grundus?" said Hornie Grundy teasingly. Hornie was Mundus's long-abiding faithful wife and had been married to Mundus for almost two centuries (they got married when they were a sweet 250 gnome years young). What's more, Hornie knew when something was troubling Mundus. And she was also the only one who could get away with calling him by his pet-name, Grundus.

"I got some icky-arr between my toes again," said Mundus.

"You can't icky-arr me, Grundus. I know when your gnome mind is grinding overtime," said Hornie in a playful yet concerned voice.

"No, really." Mundus shrugged as he pulled a chunk of dark, dirty fluff from between his big toe. "Look, a wretched piece of icky-arr right there!" Hornie frowned, clearly not amused. Right then a shimmering, glowing disk materialized in front of Mundus. Mundus squinted as the bright light fuzzed just a few feet away. Mundus knew immediately who had just arrived. It must be something important.

"Veeza?" asked Mundus, still slightly surprised. Mundus wasn't expecting a visit from the sun-deva, the gnome ally and helper, and messenger of the Shining Ones.

"Yes, Mundus," replied a soft, firm female voice. "I have to speak with you urgently. There is trouble in the Third Realm. There has been a goblin infiltration. Too many for this to be an accident – it must be a deliberate invasion."

"Oh yeeks – bothering botherness!" huffed Mundus loudly. "So that's what those blithering gob-bellied greenie geeks were up to. How did they get it? I have the Portal guarded!?"

"This is not the issue now, Mundus," replied the iridescent voice of Veeza. "Their presence is disturbing the energy matrix and unsettling the vortexes. You need to get in there and pull them out quickly."

"What shall we do with the slimy green scoundrels?" Mundus was hurriedly putting his boots back on, icky-arr and all.

"Just contain them for now, Mundus. Everything will come back into balance eventually – that is the way of the realms."

Several minutes later Mundus was running down the great hall as fast as his sturdy hairy legs could carry him.

"Baga!" he shouted loudly. 'Call the boys out – we got goblin trouble!"

Meanwhile…Peasly was hunting for a hospital. Little did he know that hospitals are not likely to be found in small villages. Yet when it comes to size (and hospitals) the goblins are the last, and least, to know. And Peasly knew that if he couldn't find a hospital soon then he would have to find some living humans with eyes to poke out. This thought did not appeal to him, having to struggle with those pale creatures with far too much body hair and stinky breath. Just in case though, Captain Peasly had with him his nifty eye-scooper and sting-spray in his bag. Peasly's rubbery ears pricked up as he heard an "eeek eeek!" – the goblin call sign, not far ahead. His two deputies were pointing up at something on the side of a building. When Peasly arrived, he saw that it was a green neon cross flashing in the early morn.

"Look – a cross, boss," squawked one of the deputies. Peasly reached into his sack and pulled out a small book with the title *The Goblin Guide to Third Realm Things*. In the book, under **Hospital,** it read: 'Human institution for treatment of injured or sick people – often symbolized by the following cross,' and below the text was a picture of a cross.

"Is it a green cross, Captain?" asked one of the officers.

"Dunno," replied Peasly. "Zhe book is in black and white. Anyway, good enough for me. Inwards and onwards, y'hay!" Peasly hopped for the back entrance without another word and taking a goblin *wrangler* from his sack he proceeded to stick the thin metallic-looking object into the door's lock. "Zhis'll busting fix it," gurgled Peasly, just as the lock clicked and the door slid open in Peasly's claw. "Now for zhose damn stinking eyeballs!"

Back on the outskirts of Pratt's Bottom, Baga and Fender had arrived with their own squadron of gnomes.

"These are the coordinates of the last Blue Portal passage," called out Baga to his squad. "Their destination must surely be that village ahead. Spread out, find those greasy gofers, zap 'em with your stunner, pack 'em up, and haul 'em back. Do it quick, do it neat – and for gnome-sake don't let the big fellows see ya!" And off they scuttled into town, on a mission.

The Elite Goblin Squadron were sure making a mess of things. By now most of Main Street had been goblin-ized, with either spray paint, graffiti, glued-up letter and post boxes, damaged signs – well, just plain goblin-trocious! Some of the green rubber-bellies were swinging from lampposts by the time Baga and his gnome crew arrived on the scene. Now that was a surprise for the unsuspecting goblins – and *zap*! The gnomes didn't lose any time in zapping and stunning.

"Zap 'em, boys!" yelled Baga, as discreetly as he could. He was worried that any moment now the village of Pratt's Bottom would start to wake up, and the big fellows would begin to trot out of their comfortable brick houses and then…well, then there would be big trouble. The big fellows would probably go into shock as a first reaction to seeing a bunch of crazy goblins being chased by zapping gnomes carrying sacks. Then, likely, they would go into denial, which is a typical state of the big fellows whenever they are confronted with something they don't understand. You see, one of the most important rituals between the big fellows in the Third Realm is this thing called *status quo*, which basically means not wishing to know about things which do not fit into the system. Big fellows like systems and for everything to be familiar – they actually fear the unknown as much as gnomes fear snot gurgles, which is saying something. So Baga knew he had no time to waste. It was now a cat-and-mouse game. Or rather, a gnome-and-goblin game of *catcha*! Fender, being a younger gnome, was agile and quick, and he could swing too when he wanted to. And Fender just loved the idea of zapping the greasy goblins. He had already zapped four goblins as they were spraying graffiti on the Village Hall building. Soon he had them all bagged-up in the sacks. He just didn't know what to do about the big ugly goblin faces they had painted over the front of the building. Oh well, everyone would just think it was some young kids having a joke, and every child in Pratt's Bottom would be suspected – nothing too bad.

Then something caught Baga's attention from the corner of his eye. He was sure he had seen a speck of green running into a side street. "Fender, you take charge of things here. There's something I have to check out." Baga ran off in the direction of the green blur. By the time he arrived at the side street it is empty. There was no one, no thing, or no goblin, about. As he looked around, he noticed that a rear side door had been left open. A shop with its backdoor open at this time of the morning? thought Baga. Above the door he saw a sign that read 'Pharmacy & Eye Clinic.' What the blooming blunder do goblins want with a big fellow pharmacy? wondered Baga as he proceeded to creep through the open door. He had his stunner at hand, ready to zap the first gangly green thing that came his way.

Peasly and his two officers were rummaging through the clinic looking for human eyes. "Where are all zhe ill people?" demanded Peasly.

"Maybe they all got better?" suggested one of the officers.

"Zhat's no goblin good. I need ill people, sick ones with big eyeballs ready for stealing. We have zo find eyeballs – get looking, or you'll both be put in a bath when you get back," threatened Peasly with a true captain's menace.

"Eeek!" screeched both of his goblin officers and jumped away extra quick. Everything went manic as the goblins turned the clinic upside down, pulling out drawers, emptying cupboards and throwing all the contents on the floor. Peasly was also beginning to panic now – he must find those eyes! He began jumping around like a goblin who's just eaten twenty slime-balls in a row and is so pumped up. Then…

"Captain, Captain!" shouted one of the officers from another room. "Jackpot, yee-hah!"

Peasly ran into the room and saw one of his officers leaping madly in the air and pointing towards a set of opened drawers. When Peasly saw what was in the drawers he too joined his officer in a goblin squeal, "Eeeeeeekkkkkkk, yesssssssss!" Inside the drawers were row upon row of eyes: blue eyes, green eyes, brown eyes – enough colors to make a goblin slimebow. Excitedly, Peasly started to stuff all the eyes into his bag and didn't notice that his two officers suddenly scampered off out of the room. There was a distraction somewhere outside.

In the passageway of the clinic stood Baga with two Elite Squadron goblins facing him – it was now a stand-off. Baga didn't flinch. He was not afraid of those pot-bellied, bat-eared, green rascals. He'd been around 399 years and knew enough tricks to handle those wet slime balls. For starters, Baga went into his famous *Shiko Dachi* karate straddle stance (well, it's famous in all of Grundy City). The goblins continued to look ahead blankly, not even blinking. It's not that they were incredibly brave and unfazed by Baga's posture – it's just that they didn't have a clue. And both goblins were still standing there by the time Baga had run and slid on his knees and poked his stunner right under the overhang of each one of their bellies. The goblins collapsed like rubber blobs upon the floor. Baga grabbed them by their feet and scooped them into his large sack. Then it was Baga's turn to be surprised as Fender darted into the clinic waving his hairy gnome hands in the air.

"Baga, gotta go, the big fellows police are coming! Their *eee-oor* cars are in the street."

"Damn it," grunted Baga with an almighty huff. "Those brainless goblins must have set the alarm off." At that moment a grinning Peasly entered the passageway with a bulging bag strapped over his shoulder. "Here, take this sack and get these goblins outta here. I'll meet you back in the Second Realm," urged Baga.

Fender knew better than to argue with a good idea. He scooped up the sack with the goblins inside and was out of the place quicker than Peasly could think.

"What's in the bag, goblin?" Baga put on his best gruff voice. Peasly tried to put on an innocent face as he rolled his goggle eyes upward.

"Oh, just some slime balls I packed for lunch," he snorted.

"You're lying – you're the slime ball. What for the gnome-life of me do you goblins think you're doing here?" demanded Baga as he got ready to perform another slick karate position.

"Oh, we're just on vacation." Peasly smiled as he waved to something behind Baga. Luckily, Peasly didn't have to worry about thinking up his next excuse as circumstances had come to his rescue. Baga turned around and with a look of shock on his face he saw two big fellow policemen staring down at him. His look of shock immediately turned to a look of stone. Baga had been stone-gnomed.

"Eeeek!" squealed Peasly as he slipped around the stone figure of Baga and dashed past two very startled and bewildered policemen, jabbing one of them in the buttocks as he fled. How the policemen were going to explain that to their superiors we will never know – or best not to know. Peasly was in the village main street before he realized that there were no more goblins about. The fact is, the whole gnome squad, including Fender, had returned to the Second Realm through the portal before the whole village woke up. Peasly though didn't think too much about it. No doubt he expected his Elite Goblin Squadron to have decided to go back home too – the whole disobedient bunch of them! Peasly hopped and leaped down the main street as fast as his wobbly green feet would carry him. There were now a few people beginning to open their shops for early trade. As he rushed past 'Shirley's Vegetables,' a middle-aged man squinted as he saw Peasly's mad spindly figure dashing by.

"Did ya see that, Shirley?" the man asked his female friend who was stacking boxes outside.

"Oh, it's probably just an anomaly," she replied as she rearranged the tomatoes. Peasly kept on going, a huge grin on his ugly green face and one hand on his bag of human eyes. Peasly was sure that Farnuk would reward him for such goblin-tastic work. Reaching the field where he had first arrived, Peasly found the small circle of stones on the floor that showed the location of the portal crossing. Remembering to look at the tattoos on both his arms he whispered the sacred **HOG**: heart ~ soul ~ love ~ service.

Whoosh. And Peasly kept on running – right through two startled gnome guards who were not expecting any more goblins. Zvoom…and leaping into the forest he headed straight back for Tam Tower, grinning stupidly all the way.

CHAPTER FIVE
EMERGENCY IN GRUNDUSLAND

Grundy City was in a bit of a spin. All the gnomes who lived there had now heard about the goblin incursion into the Third Realm – and they all knew this meant trouble! Not only had the rules and the order of the Realms been disturbed, so had the orderly peace in Grundusland. The whole place was in a buzz, with gnomes of all ages (but not all sizes) out in the streets talking and gossiping amongst themselves. Grandpa and grandma gnomes were wheezing and "I don't know what-ing" and "tut-tutting" about the whole commotion. Parent gnomes were speaking hurriedly and worriedly with other parent gnomes about how this confusion may affect their younger ones…whilst the young gnomes were all loving the excitement! Nothing this exciting had occurred in Grundusland since Pipher Noot had set off fireworks for fun on top of the castle and every gnome thought the Shining Ones were returning. Even the neo-primitive gnomes living 'off gnome-grid' had decided to leave the fields and come into the city to share the excitement, the gossip, and the worry. There was nothing Mundus could do but to call for an *Executive Gnome Meeting* (EGM) to discuss the problem of the goblin infiltration. All the top so-called 'executive' gnomes were called to the Council Chamber – the posh grand meeting hall in the castle. Mundus had also ordered a media blackout, which in truth only affected *Gnome News*, the single newspaper in Grundusland. Mundus was also deeply concerned about another matter, which was not yet public – where was Baga? Fender had returned, along with the other gnomes, carrying the sacks of stunned goblins. Yet Baga had yet to materialize in the Second Realm, and this was worrying Mundus who felt something was not right. That was why he had quietly called upon Veeza, the sun-deva, to look into the matter.

"So, the last time you saw Baga he had stunned two goblin officers and was facing Peasly, that weasel of a Captain?" asked Mundus, who was now talking with Fender in his private quarters.

"Yep," replied Fender as he scratched his small youthful beardy chin. "And he told me to leave with the sack before the big fellows police arrived."

"This is not good, not good," muttered Mundus to himself. The most likely thing that could have happened to Baga was now forming in his mind – and Mundus didn't like it one gnome bit. Just then the glowing presence of Veeza materialized as a hazy ball of light hovering in the room.

"Ah, Veeza, right on time!" said Mundus with a sigh of relief.

"The news is not good, I'm afraid, Mundus. It is as we suspected – Baga was stone-gnomed when the policemen arrived." The voice of Veeza, like her presence, hung in the air with a calmness and serenity. Sun-devas are able to materialize at will in all the realms and, as such, are of higher intelligence and serve the greater good. The gnomes of the Second Realm had always had an honored connection with the sun-devas, as a gift for their service to the Shining Ones. And Mundus Grundy had come to know Veeza on many occasions and trusted her without question.

"Baga has been taken from the pharmacy where he was found and is now in the local police station. They are keeping him in a storeroom as the only piece of evidence," continued Veeza.

"Mmm…then we will have to mount a GRALE as soon as possible," sighed Mundus. "And what in the name of gnome sanity are those green gofers up to over in Tam Tower? Veeza, would you be able to do a spying mission for us to find out what the goblins are up to?"

"You know, Mundus, I cannot," replied Veeza in her calm and gentle voice. "We must allow the natural forces of balance and disruption to play out. We cannot interfere with this process in your own realm. However, you can ask this of another. Why not ask Neem, your sprite-helper, for her assistance in this matter?"

"Great idea!" agreed Mundus. At that moment a round little gnomish face half-covered with yellow locks of hair peered in from the doorway. It was Serly Frundy, Mundus's well-known and popular niece. Serly was well-liked amongst the other gnomes not only for her attractiveness but also her cleverness and practicality. Mundus nodded permission for Serly to enter the room. Gnome Fender could not help blushing as she walked past him.

"The *Executive Gnome Meeting* is ready to begin, Mundus," said Serly in her usual confident voice.

"Good. I have some plans," replied Mundus with a smile.

*****

And the plans were agreed – a GRALE rescue immediately, led by Serly Frundy, with Jompa and Fender in assistance. No more than three gnomes, otherwise it was too risky. And besides, a GRALE rarely had more than three gnomes anyway: two gnomes to carry back the stone-gnome whilst the third to command the mission.

Meanwhile, Mundus needed to know what was going on with the goblins over in Tam Tower, which was where good old 'Spritely' Neem came in. Neem, affectionately known just as 'Spritely,' was a female sprite and friend of the gnomes. In fact, Spritely had once helped Mundas's father – Burgus Grundy – out of a pickle when he was stranded in Pukey Swamp in goblin territory and was sinking fast. But that is another story…

The closing of the *Executive Gnome Meeting* included the standard singing of the Grundusland Anthem (see **BOGGLE** - Appendix), which drove Serly to gnome-boredom as usual. Shortly afterwards, Mundus was back in his private quarters.

"Yip yipee!" said a high-pitched voice. A tiny, winged figure about twice the size of a large pinkle fly was buzzing and somersaulting around Grundus's head. "Love it, let's go for it. Wheee…I'm off!"

"Hey," shouted Mundus, "come on, Spritely, you must be serious about this."

"I am serious, Mundus, in an excitable yet crazy kind of way," giggled Spritely in her playful girl's voice. Spritely whizzed through the air in her fairy-like way. Like most little girls she liked to change her clothes often – only that Spritely was in fact centuries old (some sprites don't grow up, didn't you know?). Today Spritely was wearing a flamingo pink jumpsuit, with her wings poking out of the back.

"You must not be seen, Spritely. You know the score over in goblin territory," warned Mundus.

"Sure thing, Papa Mundus," teased Spritely, still whizzing about his head. "I shall go incognito!" And whoosh…out she flew with the tiniest of buzzes.

Over at Tam Tower... Peasly had run in like a gibbering maniac. He had been clutching his bag of eyes and blurting out, to every goblin he laid eyes on, that he was an "anomaly."

"I'm an anomaly, zhat's what I am, a great goblinly anomaly – zhat's what they called me!"

"I don't care what they called you, you greasy boggle-eyed fairy-seeker – where is my Elite Goblin Squadron, you stinky-finger?!" squawked an angry Farnuk as he stamped his foot on the floor. Peasly stood still in silence, exhibiting the same goblin empty-headed paralysis.

"What, are zhey not here?" he asked finally, a brainless look on his green face.

"No, they goblin ain't!" growled Farnuk. "You came back alone, you imp-pusher!"

"Eeek..."

"AHHH, sniper-dipers, Peasly – now you're a captain of no army! And my elite squadron is probably sitting in a gnome jail eating wood chippings and drinking concentrated leaf juice – urrghhk!"

"Eeek!" Peasly squirmed at the thought of it.

"Tell me at least you have the human eyes?"

"Oh yesss, sire, I got zhee eyes." Peasly grinned as he held up his bag for Farnuk. Farnuk gurgled and chuckled, and rubbed his hands together.

"Nice one...now it's time for an *All Important Goblin Meeting* (AIGM)."

The *All Important Goblin Meeting* took place in Farnuk's throne room at the very top of the dark, dank Tam Tower. It was a small gathering. Present were Wenkle Frat and

Peasly Greel, with special attendance privileges given to Bodel Nak, Kluth, and Konji. Farnuk was sitting well pleased with himself, examining his crinkly fingers in slow detail to make all the rest wait. And the rest of the small gathering was indeed waiting – very impatiently. Even Wenkle Frat, Farnuk's most trusted goblin deputy, was poking around inside his ears, and flicking the resultant gungy sticky ear mess onto the floor. Finally, Farnuk raised his hand for ceremonial silence. It was an empty gesture since the room had been silent already for quite a while. However, Farnuk was not going to let the occasion pass without exploiting it to the full. It wasn't every day that Farnuk could have an excuse to hold an *All Important Goblin Meeting* (AIGM).

"Goblins, semi-quasi friends, and mostly loyal servants, what a momentous occasion this is," announced Farnuk rather over-dramatically. Peasly's eyes squinted in the hope of better understanding just what Farnuk was saying. Everyone else merely had blank looks on their faces. And if you could see the faces of Kluth and Konji theirs would probably be blank too when having to listen to Farnuk. Farnuk sighed and rolled his goblin eyes. "Look here, mo-men-tous means it's an important occasion. Okay – got it?" At which Wenkle and Peasly sighed and eagerly began clapping their goblin hands together, not exactly knowing what else was expected of them. It really was a new state of affairs. "Yes, yes, yes; it is indeed a time to be goblin-giddy with excitement. Deviousness does await us. It is soon time to move on to the next stage of our illustrious Ignoble Plan…haha!"

"Haha!" squealed the rest of the gathering in half-unison, although no one seemed particularly convinced.

"We shall subdue those gnome-heads and conquer Grundusland once and for all," snarled Farnuk in the most guttural voice he could muster. "We shall stone-gnome them into submission. We shall decorate the Second Realm with stone-gnomes and rename it Tamerland! And I, Farnuk Tam, shall be declared Goblin King! Yeaahhhaaa!' he shouted with a triumphant punch into the dank air.

What Farnuk didn't know was that he nearly struck the silently hovering figure of Spritely, who had managed to emergency maneuver away from Farnuk's fist just in the nick of time. Spritely was in stealth mode, which meant her tiny vibrating wings made almost no noise – or rather, no noise audible to most ears. And because she was on a stealth mission, Spritely had changed into a black jumpsuit and was wearing a tiny black mask over her eyes. In the shadowy nooks and crannies of Tam Tower, Spritely could pass unseen. Now she had moved away from Farnuk and was perched on an alcove within good listening range. She could see below how the gathering was becoming excitable. Farnuk was now standing up on his throne chair and working the small crowd as best he could. Wenkle and Peasly were cheering and jeering, and Bodel was also jeering yet with a knowing smirk on his face. Kluth and Konji were, as ever, whispery in their appearance and even more whispery in their intentions. Their two smoky figures seemed to quiver as if excited – yet who could really tell? It was more likely that they were shuddering at the display of distasteful goblin antics.

"Show me the eyes! Show me the eyes!" commanded Farnuk in an exuberant squeal. Peasly, with great reverence and pride, stepped forward and placed the bag into Farnuk's hands with an almighty grin. No doubt Peasly was expecting some squad goblin promotion for this. He was, after all, the only goblin able to accomplish the mission. Then again, he was Peasly Greel, captain of the Elite Goblin

Squadron, which had just been unanimously captured. Farnuk fished his claw into the bag and brought out a fistful of eyes of all colors: green, blue, brown, and others. A quizzical frown slowly rippled across his green brow. One of his eyebrows raised up, and his tongue slipped to one side of his mouth. Yet still he said nothing. He then tapped the eyes with his nails. He even licked one or two of the eyes. Finally, he put one of them between his teeth and squeezed. Nothing. Farnuk pursed his scaly goblin lips and glanced over to where Peasly was still proudly standing to attention.

"Peasssly," hissed Farnuk in a slow drawl.

"Yesss, sire," replied Peasly with the beginning of a nervous look.

"Where did you get these eyes?"

"From a kind of little hospizal – one with a green cross," gurgled Peasly a little more nervously.

"A green cross?"

"Yep, definitely a green cross." Peasly nodded, and nodded again, and again.

"Were there any humans in this little, er, hospital?" enquired Farnuk.

"No. None."

"Not even sick ones, maybe?" Peasly shook his head. "And so, you didn't get these eyes from actual human heads?" Again, Peasly shook his head. "Mmm…so let's be clear on this. You didn't scoop these eyes out of human heads. In fact, you didn't see any humans at all. Is that right?" This time Peasly both nodded and shook his head. "And so, where may I ask, did you find these eyes?"

"In a cupboard," answered Peasly, as if it was the most obvious thing in the world.

"In a cup...board?" hissed Farnuk in a low, drawn-out whisper. Peasly nodded his head again, but Farnuk wasn't watching as he had already dropped his head a considerable few inches until it was almost resting on his belly. Then he exploded. "Sniper-dipers, Peasly, you cretinous blobfish. You're a damn idiot stinky-finger! These aren't human eyes – they're *plastic* eyes!" Everyone in the room fell even more silent, if that was even possible. Farnuk's eyes were almost bulging out of his head. If staring could ignite a flame, then Farnuk would have started a wildfire in that moment.

Peasly didn't seem to get it though, as the blank look on his face indicated. "Yesss, your great goblinness – and what is zhe problem?" Peasly shrugged and gawped.

"Problem! Problem! You bloated imp-pushing fairy-seeker; the problem is that they are not *real* human eyes! Get it? No human eyes equals no stone-gnomes. No goblin-tastic Farnuk Ignoble Plan...kapoof!' Farnuk sat back down visibly exhausted. "A snark, a snark, my kingdom for a snark," he croaked hoarsely.

"You wish us to find a snark for you?" asked Wenkle, slightly bemused.

"Ah, you illiterate slime mob! I'm surrounded by rubber-bellied infidels," cursed Farnuk. Then with a piercing stare he looked over to where Bodel Nak was still calmly standing, feigning innocence. "What do you have to say, little imp?" Farnuk pointed a scaly finger in Bodel's direction.

"Mmm...well," mused Bodel, tapping his cheek as if thoughtfully. "They may not exactly be *human* eyes, yet they are very definitely made *for* humans to be their eyes. Why should they still not work? It's all a question of programming. The gnomes are programmed to turn to stone when they see what they believe is the gaze from a human eye. Whether they are made from biological human mush

or plastic, it still functions as a human eye – does it not?" said Bodel, concealing a half smile. He was also smiling to himself inside, knowing full well that what he was saying was rubbish. Yet that was now his whole new plan. If he could persuade Farnuk to go ahead with his Ignoble Plan using the plastic eyes, then it most surely would not succeed. And the likely outcome would be that Farnuk would be captured just like the rest of his goblin squadron. And that would leave Tam Tower open for Bodel to walk into. Even he, ingenious imp as he considered himself to be, could not have planned it better. And, of course, the djinns Kluth and Konji had agreed beforehand to go along with him. The djinns, for their benefit, had agreed to do so, knowing that just having Bodel to deal with once Farnuk was out of the way would be sweet. Yet it is difficult to know just what exactly the djinns were thinking, or even up to.

Farnuk's goblin frown began to curl upwards as if he too liked the new direction of thought. "Yes, why shouldn't they still function as a human eye?" he said to himself out loud. "An eye for an eye. An eye is an eye – eye eye!" He chuckled to himself.

"Yes, yes, o noble badnacious one. We still have the plan – it is still your Ignoble Plan. And no gnome-head is going to out-goblin you, Farnuk," snorted Wenkle in full creepy mode, wringing his hands.

"Yes, quite right," said Farnuk with a prideful puff-out of his goblin belly. "Farnuk Tam is more cunning than a Ukrainian ferret; more ferocious than a four-armed fighting duck. I'm gonna put those dreamy, creamy, fluff-bearded gnomes in their stone place – ahah!" Farnuk was once again in full energy mode.

Spritely was loving this *All Important Goblin Meeting* (AIGM). She hadn't had such fun since the time she saw two snotgurgles trying to cross a river on stilts. In her excitement she was doing backward summersaults in the air, all very silently. And she was clapping her tiny sprite hands in joy as she listened to how both Kluth and Konji agreed with Bodel that in fact the plastic eyes could still work against the gnomes. It was truly hard for Spritely to suppress her fits of giggles; her little body was shaking all over. She had to get out of there soon or she would be in danger of letting out loud shrieks of laughter. Just as she was about to whizz out of the room she spotted, or rather felt, a gaze upon her. Spritely then noticed that one of the djinns – perhaps it was Konji? – had fixed some kind of energy attention onto her. For a brief moment, Spritely froze, or perhaps she was paralyzed; she wasn't quite sure. Then just as swiftly as it came, so it left. The djinn's gaze was no longer upon her. As a sprite, she knew well enough the perception, and the power, of the djinns. Yet somehow this djinn had wanted Spritely to leave, as if her presence and spying was not important. Waiting no longer, the little sprite in her black jumpsuit got out of Tam Tower faster than a gnome sneeze.

Back in Grundy City...preparations were being made for another GRALE rescue mission. Mundus may be a gnome king, yet he was an all-hands-on-deck type of gnome. Where there was work to be done, Mundus was there. This time it was even more personal for Mundus as it was Baga, his best gnome buddy, fellow smecker, and one of the best woodchucks around who had been stone-gnomed. And at this time of goblin interference and mischief making, the last thing Mundus needed was his best buddy out of the way. That was why he was heading straight for the GRALE Research Lab where his best scientist gnomes were working on the latest gnome stealth gadget. Mundus knew exactly which gnome he needed to see.

"Ah, Rundy, how are you, old chappie?" said Mundus in his best king-friendly voice.

Rundy looked up from his workbench, a pair of silver-rimmed spectacles hanging on the bridge of his nose. His very pink beard was something one could not avoid looking at. In fact, Rundy had become even more well-known because of it – not something that Rundy was himself well pleased with. He was a scientific gnome, a head full of ideas, theories, and hypotheses; he did not have time for pink beards or pink jokes.

"I think we got it this time," mumbled Rundy, as he finished messing with something on his table.

"Ah good, everything's pink then…errm, rosy I mean," said Mundus with a slight chuckle. Rundy just peered over his spectacles, clearly unamused, even if it was a kingly wisecrack. "Well, let us see it then," continued Mundus with an encouraging smile.

Rundy took something from the drawer of his worktable and, turning his back to the king, fiddled with some straps over his head. When he was ready, he turned around and faced Mundus.

"Whooh!" exclaimed Mundus, stepping back. "Don't tell me, you are an Olympic gnome swimmer?" The pink beard shook from side to side. "Okay then, a futuristic miner digging on the moon?" Mundus chuckled. Again, the pink beard gave a strong shake from left to right. "Okay, okay, I got it! You're a new breed of Jedi gnome, fighting the dark Empire." Mundus bent half-over in laughter.

"Come on, Mundus, you smecker, stop the poking and get with the program," snapped a slightly annoyed pink bearded

Rundy. Rundy was wearing a pair of extremely dark rubber goggles over his eyes that made him look like he had just stepped out of a gnome film set.

"Okay, spell it out to me, Rundy. Are these goggles something to do with helping us out in the Third Realm?"

"Right so, Mundus," said Rundy nodding. "These are state-of-the-art light reflecting goggles that have a special tint on the surface so that the part of the electromagnetic spectrum used by the human eye will not pass through. Yet we gnomes will continue to see as normal since our eyes use a different light range."

"So, you're telling me that these large dark black goggles effectively cut out the light?" asked Mundus.

"Correct-a-do," replied Rundy, tapping the plastic eye of the goggle.

"In other words, these goggles reflect back certain waves of light, so they don't enter?"

"Correct-a-do."

"And we gnomes will not be affected by the big fellow gaze and get stone-gnomed?"

"Correct-a-do."

"And so, after countless generations of gnomes, and many hundreds of stone-gnomes – why did we not think of this before?"

"That's easy," said Rundy with a smile. "No gnome scientist was ever stone-gnomed before. You see, the problem doesn't become a big enough problem until it happens to you." He stroked his pink beard. "Gnome-necessity is the gnome-mother of invention after all!" He grinned. He knew he had out-smeckered Mundus on this occasion. Nor would it be the last time.

CHAPTER SIX
HOLY GRALE!

Serly tied the belt around her dark crimson smock (a recent gnomish outdoors fashion) and brushed back her long curly blond hair. She then straightened her black skirt and looked down at her mountain boots, pulling a face of disgust.

"Black is not my usual color. It's way too dark for me, and kind of reminds me of swamp pus. But well, it's better for the security of the mission. Don't you think so, boys?"

Fender and Jompa silently nodded their heads. Jompa didn't know what to say as he knew less than gnome-nothing about clothes, especially women's clothes. What he did know about was mending and fixing broken things and clearing fallen trees and blocked rivers. It didn't matter to him what color his clothes were, as long as they fitted right and didn't have holes. On more than one occasion Jompa had been seen wearing green felt boots instead of brown. Then again, he'd never had any fashion advice in his life, or clothes sense either! Fender, on the other hand, was struck silent because he was gnome-giddy in love with Serly and was fixated on her golden locks. Likewise, he too didn't know a thing about clothes – but he was determined to learn. As soon as he got back from this GRALE mission, he told himself, he would go straight down Nobblers Avenue in Grundy City where the latest gnome fashion shops were located. Then his next mission would be to woo Serly into falling madly in love with him, so they could go off together for picnics and river swims. Fender had all these thoughts running through his head like pixie dust. He didn't even hear…

"Fender, are you ready for this?"

…didn't even hear Serly calling out to him as he was in such a reverie…

"Fender Tart – are you with me?!" called out Serly in a commanding voice. Fender snapped out of his trance and straightened up.

"Er, yep. Ready to go, sir, miss," mumbled Fender feebly. His hand unconsciously tugged at the little white beard on his face. Being a young 255 gnome years old he knew he still had a lot of beard growth years ahead of him. Youth, he felt, was surely on his side.

"I'm leading this GRALE, yet you don't have to call me sir – I'm not your male captain," said Serly in a firm yet friendly voice.

"Oh," blubbed Fender, blushing. "What should I call you then?"

"Just call me by my name, Serly. You know that we modern gnomes don't care much for rank – that's all stuffy old ways. I'm a new gnome girl!" Serly put her hands on her hips and nodded at both Fender and Jompa, who both grinned back at her.

"What's that up there?" asked Fender, pointing to the sky. Serly looked up, cupping her hand to her eyes.

"I can't see anything."

Fender giggled and slapped her on the shoulder. "Nobby-gnome, gotcha, Serly!" Serly shook her head and sighed.

"You're such a smecker!" she said grinning. They both looked over at Jompa who clearly didn't notice anything as he was too busy on his hands and knees examining a damaged flower stalk, muttering to himself.

"Everybody got their LRGs?" asked Serly. Blank looks covered both Fender and Jompa's faces. "Light Reflecting Goggles, boys!"

"Ahh," said Fender and Jompa in unison. All three gnomes proudly held up their newly prescribed GRALE gadgets.

"Great – then gnomes are go!" Serly lead the way into Octagon Lodge and activated the Blue Portal for yet another Holy GRALE – this time to retrieve their comrade Baga.

If stone-gnomes could continue thinking whilst in the stoned state they would probably be asking themselves, "What the gnome-sense am I doing here?" Yet luckily – for both gnomes and the big fellows – a stone-gnome is in a form of suspended animation, or concrete hibernation. It's an ancient failsafe method that was created by the Shining Ones to make sure the gnomes could continue to operate in the Third Realm without damaging the big fellow's belief systems. Hence, a gnome can never be seen as a 'live' running, jumping, laughing gnome – only as a stone decoration. This keeps the big fellows happy in their ignorance that they are the only 'thinking' creatures on the planet. All this is a big joke with the gnomes of course. Then again, the big fellows are not known for their 'correct thinking.' If anything, it's the opposite. And the gnomes have a duty and responsibility; and they are needed more than ever when the so-called 'custodians' of the Third Realm are goofing everything up.

For now, Baga was standing stone still in the storage room of the local police station in the village of Pratt's Bottom. And it seemed that no one knew quite what to do with him. One of the officers suggested painting him all blue and making him a police mascot. Another officer offered to take him home for his children and put him in the back yard. Yet, at the end of the day, Baga had to remain in the storage room as he was, presumably, still police evidence. It's just that the police were not at all sure what type of 'evidence' the stone-gnome was. A break-in at the local pharmacy and eye clinic, some plastic eyes stolen, and two police officers who thought they saw a green bouncing object rush past their feet? Then there was all the graffiti that, as if coincidentally, appeared the same morning around Pratt's Bottom. And no one saw or knew anything. It was all very strange. You could say it was stranger than a doughnut being square. Yet things were not yet finished. Gnomes do not leave their brothers – or sisters – behind.

Serly scanned the horizon through her LRGs. As always, it was the dark of night when gnomes ventured into the Third Realm. Yet one of the gnomes' advantages was that they could see very well in the dark. Fender, also wearing his LRGs, leaned over to Serly.

"It's dark, isn't it?" he whispered softly.

"Of course," replied Serly. She looked at Fender as if he was losing his mind.

"These must be very good goggles – they've reflected all the light!" Fender giggled, and poked Serly in the ribs.

"You're such a gnome-head, Fender Tart," said Serly, trying to hide a smile. Jompa was several meters behind hugging a tree trunk.

"Come on, guys, this is a GRALE. No, it's a holy GRALE." Serly quickly regained her seriousness. "We've got business to attend to. We're not going to mess up on my watch. Follow me." Serly crept alongside a hedge until she arrived at a field gate that opened onto a road. The other two gnomes trotted behind her quietly, with gnome concentration. Fender was impressed with Serly's show of command, authority and, especially, discipline. Yes, he liked the discipline under Serly. Then again, he would be happy with just about anything Serly did or said at this point. She could tell him to paint his face red for extra camouflage and he would still think it was a good idea. No, he'd probably think it was a great idea!

The three gnomes climbed through the slots in the field gate and scampered over to a bunch of trees near to where the village sign stood, welcoming visitors to Pratt's Bottom. Crouching low behind the trees, Serly pulled out a gadget from her GRALE issued belt and touched some buttons on it. Fender tried to peer over her shoulder.

"It's a GPS – a Gnome Positioning System," whispered Serly as she looked into Fender's inquisitive young face. "We can locate almost any gnome in the Third Realm with this thing. Oh, don't ask me how, just trust me on this one."

"What about using the infra-energy gnome specs?" asked Fender. "That's how we located Rundy before."

"Good question, Fender, but not sharp enough," replied Serly with a knowing smile. Fender didn't know whether to blush, feel offended, or do a male pout. "The infra-energy gnome specs are good for locating gnomes when they are outside. Yet for this GRALE we need to find a stone-gnome that is locked away indoors. That's why we need the more specialized GPS. The police station must be at the other end of the village, according to this signal. Okay, boys, we will have to move swiftly and stealthily."

"Yes, Serly, swiftly and stealthily," replied Fender grinning.

Serly wasn't sure if he was serious or trying to mock her – such were gnomes!

Jompa began to walk slowly forward, placing his feet one before the other. "Swiftly and stealthily," he mumbled, as if walking on eggshells.

Serly shook her head, wondering how the male gnomes had ever got anything done!

The three plucky gnomes followed the road into the village, staying close to the bushes and hedgerows for security. Some nocturnal owls hooted as the gnomes passed nearby. Owls have always been the announcers of strange visitors to the Third Realm. Whenever a non-human visitor is nearby, an owl will hoot to signal their presence. Luckily for such visitors, the big fellows have no knowledge of this and, like most things, just ignore the hooting of owls in the darkness. The four-legged creatures though are a different matter. The odd night prowling dog tends not to disturb the gnomes. If anything, they come to sniff them out and lick them. Gnomes have a friendly relationship with dogs; and with foxes too…and with badgers, rabbits, moles, and so forth. Well, with almost all creatures, both woodland and urban. Gnomes just love other beings and creatures – it's just those damn cats that are the problem! There's something about the gnome presence – or is it smell? – that cats just don't seem to like. The result is that when you get a cat and a gnome together, you're most likely going to have a clash. And as it happens, Pratt's Bottom is a village that is not short of a cat or two.

After a short time, Serly and her gnome rescue team arrived at the edge of a park, located near the center of the village. Serly raised her hand to indicate a stop, as if sensing trouble. All three gnomes crouched down; their LRGs strapped to their faces like midnight swimmers.

"What is it?" asked Fender quietly.

"I don't like this wide-open space," replied Serly. "It's too easy for an ambush." On hearing this, Jompa let out a low moan.

"Why would we get ambushed?" asked Fender, shrugging his gnome shoulders. "We're in the middle of the night, no one is around, and no one expects us to be here. It's a simple gnome rescue, a standard GRALE."

"Nothing is ever simple in the Third Realm," muttered Serly. "You male gnomes may think in straight lines, but we girls think in curves and wavy bends. And what I see here is a bendy curve."

Fender pulled on his little gnomie beard. 'Mmm…bendy curve,' he mumbled under his breath. He then looked over at Jompa, who rolled his eyes back at him. Fender wasn't sure if Jompa would know a bendy curve from a baseball bat. But that wasn't quite the issue right now, and baseball was the fourth from last thing on their minds.

"Another thing," whispered Serly to her team, "this is a park, and parks attract things. Pleasure does that in the Third Realm. You might not notice it, yet places of fun attract both good and bad energies. And here, at night, I think we have to be careful of the not-so-good energies." Serly looked at Fender and Jompa for some kind of acknowledgment.

Fender nodded in agreement; he couldn't believe how wise Serly was. Besides, of course, also being super-gnome pretty. "Yep, for sure, parks can be dangerous places for gnomes," he said, smiling at Serly.

Jompa was now nodding too, whilst picking his hairy gnome nose.

"Mmm…I wonder what Mundus would do," Serly said quietly to herself. Her youthful gnome eyes squinted into the darkness ahead as if trying to catch the slightest sign of danger.

"Are we expecting trouble?" asked Jompa, leaning forward and pushing his full-beardy head alongside Serly.

"Anything can happen in the Third Realm. Uncertainty and the unexpected are the features of this place. It's a wobbly realm full of oddities and quirks, and peculiar energies. That's why we gnomes are always looking after the place." Serly looked at her two gnome comrades with a mixed feeling of apprehension and gnome-adrenaline.

"So, what's the plan, Serly?" Fender seemed eager to know the next move. Serly adjusted and tightened her LRGs to get prepared.

"We're going in – prepare to be flexible!" Serly then crept forward keeping low to the ground. Fender and Jompa followed on her flanks, copying her low position. They made their way over a slight rise and began to cross the open grassy park. On the other side was a playground for children, with such things as swings, slides, building frames, and a roundabout. Serly pointed to the playground and indicated it as their destination. The three gnomes, with their LRGs strapped around their heads, looked like suspicious mini-miners on a midnight stroll as they crossed the open plateau of the park with gnome-nimble footsteps. Another owl hooted as the moon slipped behind a sheath of cloud. A blanket of darkness seemed to envelope Pratt's Bottom with an eerie silence. Serly suddenly stopped and cocked her head as if sniffing the air. She turned her head sharply and scanned the horizon to her left.

"Bothering boot-straps!" she hissed.

"What's up?" asked Fender in a low whisper as he crouched beside Serly. He was feeling both a little nervous and excited to be so close to Serly amidst this adventure. He rubbed his shoulder against hers as if it was just a normal contact. Jompa crouched behind then and cracked his knuckles.

"Look over there." Serly pointed to the edge of the park to the left of them. "There's some heat movement. The goggles are picking up various small objects moving in."

"Natural night movement?"

"No, they are in formation."

"Not doobie-good," muttered Fender.

"Let's keep moving." Serly waved the team forward once more, keeping her vision focused on the left horizon.

"Picking something up on the right," whispered Jompa suddenly. All heads shifted their line of vision to the right.

"This is not gnome-good," said Serly under her breath.

"How not gnome-good is it?" asked Fender. His little heart was beginning to pound faster against his chest.

"They're all in formation and…"

"And?"

"And?"

"And they're moving in fast – RUN!" shouted Serly as she suddenly accelerated into a sprint. All three gnomes dashed madly across the open park as the enclosing objects moved in fast from both sides.

"What are they?" Fender's little legs were going like the clappers under him.

"Cats. And they're out to get cat-lucky tonight. It's a gang trap!" Serly was looking in all directions as she saw the dark feline shadows darting towards them.

"Where's the gnome cat-a-pult when we need it!?" roared Jompa from behind as if it was a question not expecting an answer.

"Just make for the swings – I have a plan!" It was time for Serly to act like a real GRALE leader.

Serly, Fender, and Jompa, like three dark glitches in the night, were scampering to the play area faster than rabbits on laxative. Around them an army of cats were closing in with hissing taunts and threatening meowing. The gnomes knew they were in cat territory now and the cats were less than well pleased, to say the least. This was not going to be the time for late night negotiations or for passing the cat peace pipe.

With an artistic leap all three gnomes hurled themselves into the air and landed each of them on a separate swing – luckily, as there were only three swings anyway! Standing on the swings they then began to push with their little feet until they were swinging seven feet in the air back and forth.

"What's your plan?" shouted Fender, seriously nervous that an onslaught of cats was gathering around the swings.

"That was it – to get to the swings," called back Serly.

"Duuhhh." Jompa groaned, and bent his knees to push harder, making another great swing.

"But how long can we keep swinging for?" asked Fender grimacing. He was hoping, of course, that he wasn't grimacing too much as it was not attractive to a fellow female gnome. He had only wanted to make a constructive yet charming grimace rather than a complaining or panicky one. He wasn't sure if he had succeeded at all. He decided then it was best to leave the grimacing to Jompa and to stick with the positive eye contact.

"Don't worry though, I'm close to a Plan B," said Serly with a smile, as she also pushed down hard to maintain her high swing altitude. Below the swinging gnomes more cats were gathering and appeared to be sitting serenely as they licked their paws and purred in delight. A big blue cat then strutted to the front and sat ahead of the others.

"That big fat blue cat must be the leader," shouted Jompa.

"You mean the muscular British shorthair?" replied Serly, trying to be as accurate as possible.

"Yup, that's the geezer," replied Jompa with a nod. The big blue cat flashed a set of orange-yellow eyes and sneered at Jompa.

"So, what's this Plan B?" Fender looked across at Serly, hoping something would come to the rescue of his knees before they began to ache.

"It's all about being flexible and improvising with the moment," called back Serly above the squeak of the swings. Fender smiled and attempted to give Serly what he thought was an attractive and brave conspiratorial nod. Yet inwardly he groaned. Sometimes female intuition just didn't make sense to him.

"I have a Plan C!" called out Jompa as he swung hard on the other side of Serly.

"What's that?"

"Well, tell me your Plan B first!" All three gnomes were now pushing harder than ever on the swings, hoping that the structure wouldn't topple over.

"My plan is that we split up and lead the cats away. Fender, you will make for the roundabout and take some cats with you. Jompa, you get to the seesaw, and I'll run over to the slide. And when we are all in position, we'll do what gnomes do best – gnome improvise! What's your plan, Jompa?"

"Urrghh. I think we'll go with your plan for now," replied Jompa with a grimace.

Now that, thought Fender, was a real grimace. Lucky for him it was Jompa that made it.

"On my mark," called out Serly. "One, two, three – gnome jump!" Now gnomes are nimble when they wish to be; they are of course used to climbing trees, mountains, and swimming in white river rapids. So, jumping from swings was an easy thing for them, and they made it look so smooth. All three of them landed on their feet, except that Fender thought it appropriate to follow through with a tactical commando roll, perhaps more for the benefit of Serly than for strategy. Then, with a howling hoard of cats behind them, each gnome ran for their allotted structure. Fender grasped the bars of the roundabout and began pushing with all his gnome strength. In no time the roundabout was spinning with Fender running along with it. He then jumped on at the same time a dozen or so cats also jumped on to follow him. The cats immediately knew their mistake and let out a mighty cat-choir of shrieks as they dug their nails into the wooden floor of the roundabout to hold on as it spun faster and faster. Fender laughed and blew out his tongue as he saw the cats pinned to the floor with a look of seasick horror on their whiskered faces. Naturally, he kept the roundabout spinning for good luck.

Meanwhile, Jompa had sped over to the seesaw and with a mighty leap had landed in the middle and was straddling it. Several cats had decided to approach Jompa from both ends, thinking the little guy would be an easy catch. Yet as they began to crawl along the seesaw from both sides he began to push down, first with his left leg then with his right. Soon it was rocking back and forth and Jompa was standing up in the middle looking like the proud captain of a ship. The cats were hanging on desperately as each side of it raised in the air before crashing down again with a deep 'thud.' Jompa, with his hands on his hips and a cool expression on his face, continued to up-down, up-down the seesaw whilst the poor cats were huddled at both ends afraid to move.

For her part, Serly had managed to reach the big slide with a train of cats hot on her trail. Without pausing, she sped up the stairs of the slide, taking each step with a little gnome leap. When she got to the top, she turned around to see all the cats likewise leaping up the stairs after her. "Come on, you furries!" she called out with a teasing wave. As the cats got near to her, she turned and plonked herself on the slide and whizzed down its slope with a "yeaahhh." As soon as she reached the bottom, she took out a gnome-sack (GRALE standard issue) and opened it as all the cats, one after the other, came sliding down the shoot and straight into the waiting sack. "Thank you very much," said Serly as she tied the top of the sack as the last cat slid in.

By the time Serly arrived at the roundabout, Fender had already stopped the whirling and was looking at the pile of cats flopped on the floor, sick as seasick puppies. "Sack 'em up," ordered Serly with a proud smile. Soon, the both of them were at the seesaw where Jompa was still standing stoutly atop the structure, slowly wobbling from side to side. At both ends, huddled on the seats, were a sad bunch of scared cats with a glazed look in their eyes. "Sack 'em up," called out Serly. As she turned around, she saw about fifteen yards away the large male British shorthair, sitting calmly on the grass at the edge of the playground. They both looked at each other for a time, and Serly thought she saw the cat smile at her – or was it a grimace? The British blue then got up and strolled calmly away. The face-off in the park had been a test for both the gnomes and the cats. Yet Serly was sure this would not be the last time they would encounter each other. She had a feeling she would meet the large male blue British shorthair at another time. Yet for now, they had three sacks of cats and a GRALE mission to accomplish.

*****

The three gnomes, each carrying cat-sacks on their backs, stealthily made their way down Main Street, dipping in and out of doorways to make extra sure they would not be seen. Finally, they arrived to where the local police station was, and to where poor Baga was in stone-gnome storage.

"Are we just going to walk in there?" asked Jompa. He scratched his bushy bearded chin with gnome uncertainty.

"We can't just walk in there, Jompa" whispered Fender. "They'll be big fellows on duty at places like this – right, Serly?"

Serly nodded her head thoughtfully. "I'm afraid so. We can't be too obvious; then again, we shouldn't be too devious either. We should stick to the gnome way of doing things according to **GRODA**." She looked at the blank faces of both the male gnomes beside her. "**GRODA** – remember?" Again, blank stares, as if the world had just frozen or both gnomes had just undergone instant gnomo-lobotomy. "It's our **G**nome **R**ule **O**f **D**irect **A**ction: 'It is unnecessary to do more things when something can be accomplished with fewer.'" Still, the lobotomy-induced state continued. Serly huffed. "Okay, it's also known as **GWID** – the **G**nome **W**hen **I**n **D**oubt law. You know, the one that goes, 'The simplest route is often the most effective.'"

"Ahh, of course – the **GWID**!" exclaimed Fender and Jompa together.

"I thought you were going a bit weird there for a minute," said Fender with relief. Serly shook her head and sighed.

"Male gnomes – keep it simple, Serly," she said to herself under her breath.

"So how simple do you want it, Serly?" Jompa asked casually. "Straight in, straight out?"

"Exactly," replied Serly. "Look, these big fellows have their attention onto other things. That which we are after – our gnome brother Baga – is right under their noses and what they least expect. To them he's just a funny looking piece of stone, an odd decoration. And we have to exploit their lack of attention."

"Serly, you're just one gnome-tastic girly," said Fender with his best gnome wink. Serly turned away to hide a smile.

"Keep it focused, brother gnome, we're on a GRALE here," Serly said as she gave Fender the gnome-thumbs up. It's always wise to keep discipline with a sense of friendship, thought Serly. She then looked over at Jompa, who gave her back two gnome-thumbs up. Well, Serly was glad to see that no one seemed remotely worried about failure.

"This is the plan – we cause a distraction for the big fellows, then break into the storage room and sack-up Baga and get out of there gnome-quick. Any questions?"

"How do we know where the storage room is?" asked Jompa.

"How do we cause a distraction?" asked Fender.

"We've got no more sacks for Baga, they're full of cats!" grumbled Jompa.

Serly had to smile at the boys. After all, they were still learning – in male gnome time. "Follow the **GRODA**, guys!" She got out her GPS and after a minute or two she had located the whereabouts of the storage room. "Lompa, get your toolkit ready, we're going to be picking a lock soon. Now, time to let the cat out of the bag – or rather, the cats out of the sacks. Major distraction coming up!"

Serly, Fender, and Lompa each took their sacks and crept up to the front door of the police station. Serly then climbed up onto Fender's shoulders, who himself was standing on Jompa's shoulders, to peek through the door window. "No one at the front desk right now, it all seems very quiet," Serly whispered down to the others.

"Not surprised, what big fellow wants to be out of bed at this time of the night," said Fender looking up. Then to his great surprise he just realized that he was seeing up Serly's long black skirt. It was dark in there and he couldn't see a thing, but that wasn't the point. Fender had just suddenly had an epiphany that he was in gnome paradise, and that was enough. The next thing he knew he was falling through the air with Serly coming down on top of him…and bam! Three gnomes in a heap.

"What the huffing gnome-heads are you guys doing!?" wheezed Serly with a shocked look on her face. Fender looked over at Jompa, who just shrugged. 'C'mon, action now, before it's too late," urged Serly as she scrambled back on her feet. She then nipped in through the front door with her tied-up sack of cats. Fender and Jompa followed her with equal agility and speed. Once inside, all three of them crouched below the front desk and untied their sack of cats. They shoved the cats out unceremoniously with force and then dashed underneath a low bench at the side of the lobby.

"What's all that noise about?" boomed a voice. A policeman stepped into the center of the room at the same time all the cats began to screech and meow in high-pitched panic. Some of the cats instinctively jumped up at the policeman whilst the others, seeing the front door closed, went racing off down the corridor into the interior of the police station. "Hey!" bellowed the policeman as he tried to pull some of the cats off his legs whilst attempting to follow the others down the corridor.

"Now!" commanded Serly, as she ran out. Fender and Jompa dashed out from under the bench and, following Serly's lead, ran down the same corridor as the cats until they reached the second door on the right. Serly pointed to it and Jompa flicked out a long, thin metallic object from his tool belt and fiddled with the door's lock. In about five seconds the door swung open, and they all ran in. Serly already had her flashlight on and was scanning the room. "Baga!" she called out as she spotted a stone figure in the corner. Without a word, both Fender and Jompa scurried over, put a sack over their stone-gnome buddy and lifted it onto their shoulders. They then dashed past Serly and hurried towards the front door. Serly followed them as she heard a cacophony of sounds and squeals and yells behind her that sounded like a game of cat football was in play. Out the front door they ran and back the way they came down Main Street of Pratt's Bottom, without stopping for anything.

"Just keep running – head back for the entry point!" yelled Serly from behind.

"What about stealth?" called back Fender.

"We're done with stealth, just run like the clappers!"

"What if we're seen by the big fellows?" shouted Jompa, one end of the sack over his shoulder.

"Doesn't matter for us – we're wearing LRGs!"

"Rock on, Rundy! Yeehaa, gnome-home here we go!" squealed Fender.

The three gnomes, two of whom were carrying a sack between them, ran madly across the park and back towards the field and the small stone circle that was their portal for the Second Realm. If anybody happened to be up and about in the early hours of the morning it would be doubtful if they could've seen anything anyway. The three gnomes, all fifteen inches of them, were dashing so fast in the dark night that people of the Third Realm would have likely mistaken them for three mad badgers on the run. In no time at all, Serly, Fender, Jompa, and stone-gnomed Baga were approaching the portal. Jompa could hear Fender close to him chanting the Holy Oath of a Gnome – the **HOG** – that was their access back home. Well, it was not exactly that far away really, just a slight vibrational adjustment.

"Afraid you might forget the **HOG**?" called out Jompa as he huffed and puffed.

"Nah," wheezed Fender, "but just making gnome sure – for Baga's sake." At that moment something moved ahead, a dark figure right in front of their line of direction. Jompa spotted it first and shifted into a slow jog before halting. Fender almost ran into him, as did Serly as she came up fast from behind.

"What the holy gnome is going on?" asked a clearly annoyed Serly. Jompa pointed ahead of him, and that was when both Fender and Serly saw the dark figure, licking its paws. "Urghh," groaned Serly as she recognized the outline of the big blue British shorthair. "Don't these cats have anything better to do?" Fender and Jompa just shrugged as if the question were directed to them.

"What are we going to do now?" Fender asked in his high-pitched voice. Both male gnomes looked at Serly for guidance.

"Female gnome power is the only answer to such pesky persistence," replied Serly as she carefully eyed up her opponent. The big blue and Serly locked eye contact. "You both take Baga and go around the side until you reach the portal. The big blue isn't interested in you guys." Fender and Jompa protested but Serly shrugged them off. She clearly knew that this was between the big blue and herself. She moved towards the big, fat shorthair cat as Fender and Jompa crept around to the left to reach the portal from the side. The big blue stopped licking his paws and let out an arrogant "meowww." He then arched his back and straightened his tail before beginning to creep slowly in Serly's direction. When they were about five meters apart they both stopped and squared up to one another. Serly winked at the big blue and stuck out her tongue. "Come and get me, fat boy!" The big blue snarled and looked as if he was sticking out his tongue back at Serly. "You pompous furball," muttered Serly as she began running toward the cat. The big blue leapt forward at Serly as she got close, his claws extending out from his paws. Yet he clearly wasn't expecting Serly to do a gnome ground commando roll…

*****

Serly smiled to herself as the GRALE team stepped out of the Octagon Lodge back into Grundusland. It was surely good to be back, away from the chaos of the big fellows and their fears and paranoia. Yet most of all, it was good to have Baga Gheet back home. Serly was very, very relieved, and also felt a pleasant warm tickling sensation inside her too.

Oh…and in her right hand she was clutching the tail of something that was furry, blue, and very, very stiff.

CHAPTER SEVEN
PLOTS WITHIN PLOTS

Mundus Grundy strolled through the palace gardens in deep thought, his hands tucked behind his back. His wife Hornie was picking flowers nearby for her basket. Mundus walked over to her and put his hand gently upon her shoulder.

"Things are never still in our worlds, my dear," said Mundus with a sigh. Hornie looked up at Mundus and smiled.

"It's the nature of change and growth. That's how the Realms work. We've always known that," Hornie said gently.

"Ey, we've known that over countless generations. Yet to where this change takes us, we cannot know. Perhaps only the Shining Ones have that knowledge."

"What's troubling you today, my sweet dear woodchuck?" asked Hornie sympathetically.

"Well, it's these recent incursions into the Third Realm. I think it means something else is coming," replied Mundus quietly.

"Like what?"

"We gnomes have been looking after Third Realm issues for generation after generation – my parents before me, and their parents, and the rest of the Grundy line. We go in and we fix problems such as unstable energy vortexes, nature blockages, and the rest. The big fellows in the Third Realm don't have a clue about the other Realms that exist within the same Earth space. They live in their collective amnesia, creating silly ideas and myths around any anomaly they don't understand. They live in their status quo and life just goes on. Yet now, there is something different on the horizon. Ahh…my sweet Hornie, I feel we gnomes must be prepared for changing times." Mundus picked up a flower from Hornie's basket and turned it around in his hand. "One day our son Fergus Grundy will come back to us. And he will inherit a different relationship between the Realms."

Hornie stood up and put her hand around her husband's waist. "Yes, my dear. Fergus will come back to us, and there will be a different future for him. Perhaps he will be the one to unite the Realms, as it was before."

"Perhaps." Mundus smiled softly. "The day the Third Realm wakes up is closer at hand. And the goblins are sure doing their bit. The big fellows might be able to ignore stone-gnomes popping up in their gardens but what are they going to do with rampaging green pot-bellied rascals?!" Mundus shook his head.

"All things must change," Hornie said and pinched Mundus in the belly. "That's what makes life so much fun. Now, go and be a dear and get some firewood for the stove."

"Yes, all things must pass – shall never last," said Mundus with a raise of his hands as he strolled off, waggling his gnome bum at his wife.

Whiizzz…a whirling spiral of stardust appeared in the air above Mundus's head as he was placing a bundle of wood into the corner of the kitchen. Spritely Neem did one of her aerial somersaults and then proceeded to do what looked like a disco dance when she was eye level with Mundus. Spritely was back wearing her favorite bright flamingo pink jumpsuit.

"Ah, Spritely!" chuckled Mundus. "I see you've not lost any of your groove thing."

"Hey, Mundus, I'm a full-on disco diva – check this out!" Spritely then did a couple of full turns and started punching the air as though she was lifting air-weights.

"Yeah, groovy. Where's the music?"

"It's all in my head, of course; that's where the music always is. I hear the grooves and disco beats all the time. What's up with you gnomies, don't you hear the rhythm?" Mundus punched the air, first with his left fist and then with his right, just like Spritely did.

"Nah, I feel like I'm ringing church bells," he replied with a chuckle.

"That's because you're sticking your bum out!" giggled Spritely.

"All right, less of the anatomy. What did you learn from the goblins at Tam Tower?" Spritely hovered over closer to Mundus and explained to him everything she had seen and overheard. She told Mundus all about Farnuk Tam's so-called Ignoble Plan and his reason for entering the Third Realm. When Mundus heard about Peasly bringing back a bag of plastic eyes he almost rolled on the floor laughing. "So that's their not-so-bright goblin plan – it sounds more like an ignoramus plan than an ignoble one!" laughed Mundus. "Well, let them bring it on. This should be fun!"

Back in one of the dark rooms of Tam Tower…two shadowy plumes of smoke were moving around. The djinns Kluth and Konji were in conversation, whispering to one another, even though it was hard to tell which one was which.

"They're all imbeciles, Kluth. They have rubber jellied brains, and they couldn't solve a two-piece jigsaw."

"So, what are you saying, Konji my dear – that we have to double-cross them?"

"Don't be so naïve, Kluth. The goblins wouldn't think twice about double, triple, or quadruple-crossing anyone if they could. They have less ethics than they have intelligence, which isn't saying much. What I'm talking about is securing Tam Tower so we can have some refuge here in the Second Realm. You know we need it, so stop being all soft on me. You'll play your part if I say you will."

"Come on, Konji dear, don't be like that. You don't need to be so pushy. I just need time to think this over."

"You think slower than a swamp slug." Konji's voice was like a low smoky groan. "If I left you to think for yourself the sun would go supernova before you had reached a decision. Look, dear, I'm only prodding you for your own good."

"Then can you prod a little more nicely?" rumbled Kluth as his foggy wisp of a figure began to get agitated.

"Stop being such a brick, Kluth! You're so passive you'd turn into a solid structure if I left you alone too long. My prodding is good for you. Now, listen to me. We're going to persuade Farnuk Tam and his cohorts to go ahead with his Ignoble Plan which is bound to fail. He'll be left at the whim of the gnomes for them to deal with. Once Farnuk is out of the way it will be easy for us to take command of Tam Tower and make a home for us here in the Second Realm."

"And what about the imp, Bodel Nak?"

"Ah, that peevish little imp. He's in it for his own good and is nothing but a mischief maker. The problem is that he's smarter than the goblins. Yet his weakness is that he thinks he's too smart. He is a nuisance, although a useful nuisance that we can use for now. Are you with me on this, Kluth? You better be!"

"Yeah, yeah, my dear. I'm with you, don't worry," replied Kluth with what sounded like a real moan.

Somewhere else in Tam Tower... Farnuk Tam stood at his chalkboard, scribbling away, whilst several squiggly diagrams and arrows already covered most of the board. Then standing back, he admired his handiwork. "Yes, yes, this is pure goblin genius. I should be given the Gobel Prize in Intelligence for this brilliance," he muttered to himself. Then adding a final arrow to the board, he blew the chalk dusk away.

"What's this Farnuk?" asked Wenkle as he entered the room and strutted up to where Farnuk was standing.

"This," said Farnuk with a face-wide grin, "is my **Human Eye Launch Protocol.**" Farnuk proudly waved his arm to show all his scribbles and shapes on the board.

"What's a pro-to-col?" asked Wenkle with a puzzled look.

"Dah, it's a set of things, you blobfish! You know, a kind of, well, sort of like a set of things to follow – get it?" Wenkle's expression didn't change. "Ah – it's a plan, a great slime plan...my **Human Eye Launch Plan!**" snorted Farnuk with a shake of his head.

"Yeah, now I get it – it's another great plan of yours with the human eyes. Well, Farnuk, it's briiilliant!"

Farnuk winced as Wenkle slapped him on the back. "Oh, sorry your mightyness," said Wenkle nervously wringing his goblin hands. "This is going to be your big time, Farnuk. You'll be the most badnacious goblin ever. I can see it now; it's a fan-goblin-tastic future!"

Farnuk puffed out his chest and grinned. "Yess, you could say that Wenkle. Indeed, you could. I'm going to stone-gnome them beardy fairy-lovers this time. This is my mostest, boldest, Ignoble plan yet!" He said it so intensely he was spitting his words.

Wenkle couldn't stop grinning inanely and wringing his hands as if he was grounding slime-rock into powder. After several moments of silent grinning at each other he finally asked, "So, what is the **Human Eye Launch Plan?**"

"First, I'm going to send a letter to old King Mundus asking for a special audience with him and all his top gnomes. I will say we need to speak about peace between us, and the return of my Elite Goblin Squadron. I will say I have come to apologize and make friends, and that I bring a gift as my peace offering. Those pastoral tree-hugging gnomes will suck it up like spring water. Hehehehehe." Farnuk gurgled inanely into his scaly hands. "Then, when I have all his top gnomies in the same room, I will unveil my goblin gift to them – a sculpture made of human eyes! When they look upon it, they will all be turned into stone-gnomes immediately…and then, pow!"

"Pow?"

"Pow! I release the Elite Goblin Squadron and together we take over Grundy City. Every gnome that gets in our way or even looks at us will be stone-gnomed because we'll be wearing a human eye on our heads."

Wenkle blinked a few times. "How will we have a human eye on our heads – will we have to grow it on?"

"Don't be goblin-daft!" snorted Farnuk. "No, remember we got that batch of headband torches for when, way, way back we had the 'Collapse Gnome Mines Plan C' where we were going to enter into the mines and sabotage them? Well, we still got boxes of them headband torches. So, we just swap the torch for the human eye. We'll be wearing head-band human eyes. Hehehe." Farnuk stomped his foot in goblin excitement.

"Eye-tastic!" shouted Wenkle jumping up and down.

Later that day Farnuk held an 'Ignoble Plan Special Meeting' in his throne room. Invited were all those with 'need-to-know' top-goblin secret clearance. Those present included the same notorious faces: Wenkle Frat, Peasly Greel, Bodel Nak, and the djinns Kluth and Konji. Strutting like a pompous green slime strudel, Farnuk explained his now titled 'Farnuk Tam's Ignoble Evil Eyes Plan.'

"Right, listen in everyone for a most important **DET** talk – **D**evious **E**xplanation **T**ime talk," announced Farnuk. Farnuk deliberately took his time to explain the diagrams and arrows on the chalkboard, whilst waving his arms about as if he was directing a goblin cliff-jumper to land. Farnuk was obviously doing his best to make the **DET** talk as pretentious as was possible. He even threw in a few, not so eloquent, pauses for effect. Bodel, Kluth, and Konji remained respectfully silent; whilst Wenkle and Peasly gurgled and grunted their approval constantly.

"And this is my Tart de Résistance…daada!" Farnuk pointed to a diagram that looked like a blob of ice cream. "This is the sculpture of eyes! It will have eyes looking out in all directions, like a slime-cake of eyes that no one can escape from. It will have a 360-degree vision. That means eyes wherever you look…eyes, eyes, eyes…and then stone, stone, stone. Ahah!" Enthusiastic applause came from Wenkle and Peasly whilst Bodel merely gave an imp thumbs up, accompanied by a sly smile that was as much for himself as for anyone else. Low moans came from the two djinns, which Farnuk took as a sign of great approval. "Good. Then it's settled. Bodel, you are tasked with creating the eye sculpture, while I will withdraw to think over my most illustrious letter of apology to the gnome beardies."

Back in Grundy City... Baga Gheet ran down the corridors of the castle, so fast he nearly knocked over pink-bearded Rundy as he turned a corner.

"Watch out, Baga! This isn't a racecourse," grumbled Rundy.

"But I feel like a racing-gnome," called back Baga as he scampered on and up the staircase towards Mundus's private quarters. "There you are, you smecker!" he shouted as he burst into the room where Mundus was reading the daily edition of the *Gnome News*.

Mundus leapt up in surprise when he saw Baga. "Smecker you too, nobby-gnome!" Mundus and Baga belly bounced off each other and landed on the floor laughing. "So good to have you back, Baga. Where would Grundusland be without you?"

"Maybe vibrating in the Fourth Realm where everything is ...sooo...sl...ow...' said Baga, chuckling.

"Yah, we're not there yet, thank Gnome!" Mundus grinned as he poked Baga in the belly. "But maybe the goblins are going to be heading to the Fourth Realm before too long."

"Oh, don't talk to me about those slimeballs. They're like green bats with legs, but with less brains!" Both gnomes pulled themselves up from the floor laughing. "I still would like to know what they were doing in a clinic in the Third Realm – were they looking for a health check-up? What they need is a brain scan more like!" At that moment the door pushed open and Serly rushed in. She stopped abruptly as soon as she spotted Baga in the room. A small blush appeared on her cheeks, which she hoped had not been seen.

"What is it, Serly?" Mundus was still grinning as he brushed down his clothes.

"Oh, I just heard a lot of noise. I thought maybe…er…"

"Maybe that the goblins had got in?" said Baga with a wide grin. Serly smiled back and shuffled her feet. She felt like a young girly-gnome again. "Hey, thanks for getting me out of there. You commanded the GRALE spectacularly, from what Fender and Jompa say."

"It was my gnome pleasure," said Serly, this time with an all too obvious blush. Baga suddenly noticed the sweetness in Serly like never before. He had known her for many gnome years yet had never paid much attention to her as a female gnomie. Perhaps things were different now? Mundus placed his hands on Baga's shoulders as if he understood his thoughts.

"Yes, we can all thank Serly and her GRALE team for bringing you back. Now things are going to change. We have to prepare for a goblin invasion, here in Grundy City."

"What in the name of holy gnome is going on?!" said Baga startled.

"Serly, you take Baga for a walk and fill him in on the details," said Mundus as he slapped his best buddy on the back and grinned at Serly.

*****

A little while later Baga and Serly were strolling through the cobbled lanes of Grundy City. After all, it's not a very large city, and everyone walks anyway. The best form of transport in Grundusland is gnome-legs, with one placed before the other. Curiously, beside Serly trotted a big blue furry cat, purring affectionately against her legs. Baga shook his head.

"I just can't believe you brought a cat back from the Third Realm?"

"Well, it just so happened that I was swinging him around by his tail as I recited the **HOG**. The portal brought him back with me," Serly replied as she stroked the purring cat.

"I'm surprised he made it into the Second Realm."

"Well, he did arrive stiff as a board. I had to take him to the gnomospital for them to sort him out. He was still vibrating at Third Realm rate. It would be like being in stasis – imagine that!"

"Urrgh." Baga shrugged his stocky shoulders. "He probably thought he was stuck in some frozen dream, I bet!"

"Well, it took him a little while to vibrate up to Second Realm, and to shrink down to size here. But now he seems adjusted. He's no longer a big cat now – he's been gnome-sized down." Serly gave a little girly giggle as she stroked the blue cat at her feet. "And he doesn't leave me alone. I think he wants to protect me." Baga frowned, which made Serly smile knowingly. "He's the first cat from Third Realm to live here with us in Grundusland. Isn't that something?"

"Does he have a name?" asked Baga.

"Wobin – my new pudgy puddy cat. He's as soft as a weasel brush." Serly smiled to herself as if it were a personal joke.

Serly and Baga continued to stroll through Grundy City whilst Serly informed Baga all about the Ignoble Plan as told to Mundus by Spritely Neem.

Baga could hardly keep himself from laughing when he heard about the plastic human eyes. "Every gnome in his or her right mind knows that this will not work. They know that it's not the human eye alone that turns a gnome to stone. It's all about the act of perception. It's the contact a gnome has with the human perception and belief systems. Once this connection is made it triggers a mutual response from the gnome, as if they are energetically connected. This was the 'protection protocol' the Shining Ones built into the Third Realm to protect the delicate and unstable belief systems of the big fellows. If these beliefs are tampered with, then the big fellows could lose the plot. And then more instability might occur, which would be more work for us!" Serly was impressed at Baga's breadth of knowledge. She had always been attracted to intelligence in a fellow gnome. "Besides," said Baga, as they inadvertently wandered into Churly's Teahouse, "the stone-gnome effect only works in the Third Realm. It won't work here in the Second – don't the green rubber-bellies know that?"

"Oi! What's the blue furball doing in here?" called out Churly Bender as she strutted her way over to Serly and Baga. Churly was the large, round-bellied gnome madam owner of the teahouse, and a no-nonsense type of gnome. She had been the madam of the teahouse for as long as gnomes in Grundusland could remember, and perhaps before that too. And she wasn't used to having animals creep into her clean, well-kept teahouse.

"He's not a furball. He's my pet puddy, Wobin. And he's our special guest from the Third Realm." Serly gave Churly one of her most adorable smiles.

"From the Third, eh? How'd he get here then – jump into a gnome pocket?" chortled Churly. She bent down to peer closer at Wobin, her waist bulging out like the rings around Saturn. Wobin gave a teeny squeak and hid behind the back of Serly's legs.

"I'm showing him around Grundy City. He's a stranger in the Second Realm and we have to make him welcome," said Serly with a sweet pout.

Churly stiffened up, and soon a wide grin broke out over her reddened chubby gnome face. "Okay, the wee Wobin fella can come in. Just make sure I get no Wobin wee on my floor, mind you!"

Serly chuckled and led Wobin and Baga over to an empty table near to the door (just in case Wobin needed to dash out quickly!). Baga ordered a pot of nettle tea (a popular favorite) for them both, as they changed the subject onto the risks of gnome bungee jumping. After a few minutes of discussing the possibility of doing a successful bungee jump from atop of the tallest pimple tree in Grundus Forest, who should walk into the very same Churly's Teahouse on Nocker Lane but Fender with his gnome-buddy Lompa.

"Hehehe, you're such a mega-gnome bore, Lompa," teased Fender as he poked Lompa in the belly. They both sat down at a table near the counter.

"When did you become the smecker of all smeckers?" grumbled Lompa.

"Who gnomes when?!" sniggered Fender. "Maybe when I was chopping wood near your house and saw you peeing on the herb garden."

"You did not!" snapped Lompa.

"Surely, shirley did! You're such a huffalot," said Fender with a snigger. Then he noticed Baga and Serly having tea together at the other table. Suddenly, Fender's face dropped and all signs of laughter lines melted into his youthful almost-beardless face. Fender's nose wrinkled and sniffed.

"What is it, Fender – you've gone quieter than a speechless field mouse?" asked Lompa as he fingered through the tea menu. "Mmm…something different from nettle tea today I feel. Could be oolong, diplong, chenong, or red bush pimple…mmm." Lompa continued to ignore Fender's silence. "Nah, I still think it's a nettle tea day today," said Lompa finally and crossed his arms.

"You always choose nettle tea whichever day it is. You're about as predictable as a waterhoggit," huffed Fender.

"What's got into you? Someone stolen your gnome cap?" grumbled Lompa. Fender wasn't thinking about tea. In fact, he'd just lost his thirst. Why was Serly talking to Baga? Or for that matter, thought Fender, why was Baga talking to Serly? Perhaps it was all innocent. Maybe they were just discussing seed planting times – or maybe not? Fender stood up to leave. "Where you going, Fender?" asked Lompa

"I'm not thirsty. And I think I left my money-pebble pouch on the kitchen table," said Fender as he turned away and began to shuffle towards the door. At that moment Baga spotted Fender and waved.

"Hey, gnome-buddy!" called out Baga in a friendly tone. Fender nodded his head to both Baga and Serly. "Thanks again for saving my pants back there in the Third Realm. Serly tells me you were gnome-brave." Baga gave Fender a huge smile.

"Is that what you're both talking about?" asked Fender in a low voice.

"No, not really. We were talking about bungee jumping from the top of a Pimple Tree," replied Baga, smiling even more broadly than before.

"Dahh – I knew it!" blurted out Fender as he turned away and walked out of the teahouse. "Damn gnome romantics," he mumbled to himself.

Baga and Serly looked at each other and shrugged their shoulders. "Maybe it's his male gnormones," Serly said as she sipped her nettle tea. Although she knew very well that it wasn't – female gnomes have a way of knowing more about male gnomes than they know themselves.

Somewhere around the vicinity of Tam Tower…in the dank and dingy swamp marsh where lived bog rats, fen slime, and farkdarts…not a pleasant place at all. And yet it wasn't always like this. There was a time when it used to be a pleasant forestry part of the Second Realm. When the Shining Ones banished the goblins from the Third Realm and quarantined them to the Second Realm, they had to make sure they didn't interfere with the gnomes. The Shining Ones annexed a small corner of Grundusland and let the goblins live in their own space. Farnuk Tam's ancestors didn't waste any time in assuming goblin leadership, which wasn't difficult.

Urnuk Tam, father of Vernuk Tam and grandfather of Farnuk Tam, had built the monstrosity that was Tam Tower. Soon afterwards, the green forestry and beautiful meadows began to lose their shine, and nature's pleasant smells began to fade. A new smell arrived – a stinky, rubbery smell, like the sweat that rises from a spewd of goblins. It was the energy change that started it all. The goblins energy vibration, under the Tam leadership, grew daily stickier and more putrid. Whatever thought emanations they managed to achieve from their tiny brains were full of devious little plans and sly trickeries. These nasty, peevish thought emanations trickled out into the surrounding environment and began to pollute the area around Tam Tower. As the thoughts grew more deceitful and conniving, so the undergrowth became slimier and more stinky. All the original wildlife creatures moved further away into the forest nearer to Grundy City. Then other creatures arose, as if naturally attracted to the new goblin vibrations. Now the

area around Tam Tower is a marshy bog, where everyone –
including the goblins – have to tread carefully. It pays to
know exactly where the footpaths and stepping-stones are.
And there is one creature especially who knows exactly
where these paths lie – and that's the imp Bodel Nak.

Bodel Nak was an odd kind of imp, and mischievous
beyond a doubt. Some would even call him a rogue and a
rascal – a distrustful little scoundrel. If Bodel was a part of
something, you could be sure he was up to no good. And
there he was, skipping around the bogs from stone to stone
as if he had been born there. In fact, nobody knew exactly
where Bodel arrived from or how he happened to turn up at
Tam Tower. Over time, he managed to squeeze himself into
Farnuk's company by running all his errands and sucking
up to him. Yet Bodel was wise enough not to slime his way
around the other goblins. For Bodel was not interested so
much in the other goblins that hung around Tam Tower – it
was Farnuk he had his beady impish eye on. Now Bodel
was wandering around outside muttering to himself. "When
Farnuk is out of the picture I shall be the new head of Tam
Tower…mmm…Bodel Nak will find a way to get rid of
those damn djinns. You can do it Bodel, you mighty and
clever imp. You will out-imp them all and be imperor of
this impire…jejeje."

*****

At the top of Tam Tower, in the dark throne room, sat
Farnuk on his high stone slime throne dictating a letter to
Wenkle. "Look, are you sure you're getting all this down
correctly, Wenkle? I know you can be a leaky headed
blobfish sometimes."

"No, no, I've got it all down," slobbered Wenkle.

"Okay, read it back to me. C'mon, triple sharpish."

Wenkle gurgled to clear his throat before speaking. "Ahem – *Your Mightyness Mundus, King Gnomie of Grundusland,*" he began.

"Oh, that's good, that's reeal good," interrupted Farnuk. "Yess…like that – go on!"

"It has been brought to my attention – my honorable goblin self Farnuk Tam – that some of my goblins may have mistakenly operated below our principled normal behavior recently. This lapse in goblin ethics may have been responsible for an unfortunate appearance in the Third Realm. As recognized and highly respected Goblin Leader, I must take responsibility for the lapse in aforesaid principled ethics of my goblin subordinates. I thus and therefore honor your good self with my personal presence on the end evening of this week to express regret at this episode. This invitation to accept me is gracious from both our parts. I look forward whence to you receiving me in full honors with ALL your top gnomies present on this monumental occasion of our historical meeting. Regally Yours – Honorable Farnuk Tam. P.S. Don't forget to have ALL the top gnomies present – I did say this, yes?"

"Goblin-tastic!" Farnuk rose from his throne and strutted around the room, his rubbery chest puffed out. "Now where's that flat-nosed imp Bodel? I hope he's got my eye sculpture ready, it's crucial to my **H**uman **E**ye **L**aunch **P**lan. It's got to be goblin-ready to stone-gnome them tree-huggers once and for all. This realm is for the Tam dynasty, forever and more!" Farnuk marched out of the room, leaving Wenkle grinning and wringing his greasy hands.

Farnuk burst into the room where Bodel had been assigned to work on the eye sculpture.

"Well?" demanded Farnuk. Bodel had been expecting Farnuk to arrive sooner rather than later and had already anticipated the questions.

"It's not yet ready, sire." Bodel squeezed the widest false smile possible upon his small impish face.

"Show me, show me!" insisted Farnuk impatiently.

Bodel drew away the cloth to reveal what looked like a small ice-cream blob of plastic eyes, exactly as Farnuk had drawn on the chalkboard.

"Is this it?"

"As I said, your high goblinness, it is not quite ready yet. I need to stick on more eyes before it becomes your Blob de Résistance."

"My Tart de Résistance – you impish bograt!" snarled Farnuk.

"Of course, that is what I meant – your Tart de Résistance. It will be an eye-spectacle, an eye-travaganza to stone all the gnomes into submission."

Farnuk hopped from one leg to another, slavering. "Yesss…those fairy-loving gnomes are gonna get it now!"

Somewhere else in Tam Tower…

"Are you with me on this, Kluth? You better be!"

"Yeah, yeah, my dear. I already said before, I'm with you." The low moan of Kluth could be heard drifting through the air like a rumbling sigh. The two illusive djinns were twirling like smog pollution through the dank, empty corridors of slimed stone.

"Good. Now we sit back and watch these goblin games unfold. Just you keep an eye on Bodel – and I'll keep an eye on you!"

"Yes, dear…"

CHAPTER EIGHT
THE EVIL EYES

Mundus called together another EGM (*Executive Gnome Meeting*) for the top executive gnomes in Grundusland. Well, it's actually quite hard to have *executive* gnomes in a gnomocracy. Sometimes Mundus used the word just to sound official. Or rather, to let the other gnomes know that this time it was a serious meeting – and not the boy's night-in for card games of gnome-jack or gnoker. This time the word went out that Mundus wanted his deputy Baga, and his circle of close gnome buddies and advisors, to make themselves present in the Council Chamber forthwith. That is, pretty gnome-sharpish. Baga, meanwhile, was sent off to fetch Rundy who, as ever, would be nose-deep in his work, oblivious to events in Grundy City.

Rundy, with his now characteristic pink beard, was looking intently into a microscope and didn't notice Baga Gheet entering his laboratory.

"What you looking at?" Rundy looked up, suddenly startled.

"Don't you know better than to creep up on a fellow gnome, Baga? You could have interrupted a realm-saving experiment!"

"Did I?" Baga smiled cheerfully as he walked over to Rundy's worktable. Across it were scattered papers, pencils, and an array of odd instruments that looked like they belonged to a male manicure set.

"Are you trying to de-pink your beard, Rundy?"

"Don't be ridiculous," answered Rundy far too quickly. He shuffled nervously over to his desk and began clearing things away into various draws.

"Okay, no need to huff."

"I'm actually examining scaly goblin skin, if you must know. I want to know more about these rubber-bellied neighbors of ours." Rundy scratched his pink beard as if thinking deeply on something.

"They're green, smelly, and a damn nuisance! What more do you need to know?" asked Baga with a light-hearted chuckle. "Come on, Rundy ol'boy, we have an EGM to get to."

Rundy shuffled his feet and huffed, before eventually taking off his lab jacket and following Baga to the Council Chamber. When they arrived, they saw that Serly, Fender, Lompa, Jompa, and several other close gnome friends of Mundus (including Turdy Frump, Dundus Perky, and Purdy Grumpus) were already there. Also present was Mooley Myrkle, analyst on gnomocracy and advisor to Mundus. Even the hotshot female greatest mud-ball thrower of all Grundusland, Welma Wurdy, was in attendance, muscles and all. Things must be serious…

Mundus called the EGM to order, as Spritely hovered to the left of his head wearing a fuchsia-colored jumpsuit as if to mark the austerity of the occasion. All the gnomes were seated on low wooden benches made from the finest pimple trees of Grundusland forest. Every gnome was silent, waiting for Mundus to speak; even Spritely Neem had turned down the 'buzz-factor' audio on her wings.

"Fellow gnomies and gnome helpers, we have a situation arising that we must deal delicately with. The goblins of

Tam Tower, under the influence of Farnuk Tam, have decided it is in their interests to form some sort of attack against us." All the gnomes in the room simultaneously started to huff. Mundus raised his hand to silence the gnome huffing before it could rise to a crescendo. "Yet fear not, fellow gnomies. This plot is going nowhere and will not harm us. It is just the latest in brainless goblin mischief, which is all part of what they do. It is in their nature, just as it is in our nature to take care of the Realm and her energies."

"But why do the goblins have to be so anti-everything?" asked Serly, shaking her head in disbelief. Spritely whizzed over and did a few somersaults over her head to make her smile.

"It's how the Shining Ones have arranged things," replied Mundus. "It's like a law of perpetual motion – we keep the balance, they disrupt the balance. Somewhere along the way we have progress as we gnomes need to keep thinking up new ideas and innovation to keep the disruptions at bay."

"Then what about the Third Realm?" queried Baga. "When the goblins were last there it caused the local matrix to wobble. Surely the Shining Ones don't want Third Realm reality to break down?"

Mundus nodded in agreement. "That must be part of a grander plan we gnomes as yet do not know of." And saying that, Mundus produced from his pocket a brown piece of paper, which turned out to be a letter from Farnuk Tam himself, anonymously left in the king's own postbox. Mundus read out the letter to everyone, finishing with "*P.S. Don't forget to have **ALL** the top gnomies present – I did say this, yes?*"

"What's his game?" asked Jompa and Lompa both together.

"Well, thanks to the reconnaissance of our little friend here, Spritely Neem, we know exactly what their devious, so-called 'Ignoble Plan' is," said Mundus with a chuckle. Mundus then explained everything about what the goblins were planning, and more or less how they were planning to do it.

The whole room erupted in laughter. Fender couldn't stop himself from rolling off the bench onto the floor, squealing in high-pitched fits of giggles. Baga had to pick him up and put him back on the bench. All the gnomes were chuckling like woodchucks do. Some were slapping their thighs, whilst others were poking their neighbors. Even Jompa and Lompa managed to squeeze a laugh out of their usually rigid faces. Rundy, too, couldn't stop the laugh lines from creasing up and down his face like ripples on Pimple Tree Park pond.

When the laughter had subsided, Mundus went on to explain his own plan, which would include the help of their friend and intermediary Veeza, the sun-deva. Finally, after several more minutes, the *Executive Gnome Meeting* was officially closed with the usual singing of the Grundusland Anthem. Serly, rebellious as ever, only mimed the words, like the big fellows usually do in the Third Realm.

*****

The end evening of the week soon came around. And as is the way of gnomes, they were fully prepared. The Grand Reception room of Grundy Castle was lit up in the manner of welcoming a guest. All the so-called 'executive' gnomes of Grundusland were present in their best attire. Their brown felt boots were scrubbed, their green trousers pressed, and their red pointy hats all pointy. This being a special occasion, albeit a false one, the gnomes had exchanged their usual blue smocks for a range of varied colored waistcoats. These colorful waistcoats each represented the color of the gnome family, like a coat of arms, whether it be a Grundy gold and purple; a Gheet blue and yellow; or a Frundy orange and silver. Each colored waistcoat also had its own special designs and patterns, stamped from little wooden block prints. And King Mundus Grundy was wearing the only purple pointy hat, as was the right and privilege of the king – as it had been worn by his father Burgus, and by his father Rufus before him.

All the appointed gnomes were very politely, and patiently, hanging around the Grand Reception room. They were awaiting the arrival of their very special guest – the greasy, rubber-bellied Farnuk Tam. All the gnomes had been clearly briefed on their actions and what the plan was. The gnomes, including Mundus himself, were both anxious and excited. For them this was an occasion for potential fun and adventure; yet they also knew that it would not be so much fun if things didn't go according to plan. Baga Gheet, with his roundish face, was nodding over to Mundus in the hope of reassuring him. That, after all, was what deputies were responsible for. And if anything should go wrong, he was also there to protect Mundus. Not that the king would need much protection, reasoned Baga, if he could handle himself against a snotgurgle and still walk away unharmed. In comparison, the peevish antics of the green weasel Farnuk should not prove too much for the gnomes. Still, Baga felt nervous, and could not help stealing a peek, or two, over at Serly. Serly, for her part, was trying her best not to keep looking over at Baga whom, she thought, was looking gnome-handsome in his blue and yellow waistcoat. Then the deep horn call suddenly started.

The ceremonial Curlyfoo bird, a native and prized species in the Second Realm of Grundusland, began its famous siren call. The Curlyfoo bird reaches two feet high when it is standing up straight with its neck held up – which is taller than the gnomes by several inches. The Curlyfoo, with its green plumage and blue-collared tuft of hair, looks the part of a regal bird. And its large, curved flamingo-like beak can produce a foghorn nasal sound that is louder than any gnome alarm or siren. For this very reason, the royal castle of Grundusland had always used the Curlyfoo bird for any formal announcements, as you'd have to be in a gnome-coma not to be awoken by its foghorn. And that call bellowed through the hall, to signal to all those present (and beyond!) that a special visitor had arrived.

Farnuk pompously strode into the Grand Reception room as if he were a returning hero. His rubber-belly chest was puffed out and a smirk ran across his face as if he knew divine secrets (which he certainly did not!). To all the gnomes present it was obvious that this goblin was one over-confident fellow. Farnuk strut into the room as if he thought he was already king, turning his head to look at the gnomes as he crossed the center of the room and headed toward Mundus Grundy. When Farnuk was in front of Mundus he gave what could only be interpreted as a mock salute.

"Mundus, ye olde gnome king dude, what a great place you got here." Farnuk grinned, his two grey-green bat-like ears were twitching.

Mundus gave a polite nod of acknowledgement and smiled back. "Farnuk Tam, representative of the goblin spewd of Tam Tower, it is a delight to have your presence here. It has been a long time indeed."

The furrow lines above Farnuk's eyes creased. "Been so long indeed," he replied, not knowing what else to say. Farnuk was a little confused since he couldn't remember ever being in Grundy Castle before. Anyway, he didn't consider the matter important. "It's always too long from since the last we met, dear gnomie brother. What you been up to for all these moons?"

"Well, you know, hugging trees mostly," replied Mundus with a half-concealed chuckle. Right on cue all the other gnomes chuckled also, helping to break the ice. Farnuk giggled too, looking about and nodding to the room as if he was the Second Realm's greatest star.

"Keeps you gnome-heads out of mischief, eh? What do you say, eh?" Farnuk grinned even more broadly, feeling like he was directing the show.

Mundus abruptly stopped smiling, as did all the other gnomes, and leaned over towards Farnuk. "And what have you goblins been up to, I wonder?"

Farnuk continued grinning in the stony silence, which quickly turned into a gulp. "Er, well, yes, there is that small matter of our little visit to the Third Realm. Well, just some eager goblins wanting an adventure – nothing more. No harm done, eh. What do you say, Mundus buddy? Let's be grown-up about this and not let it come between us. There's much we goblins and gnomes can do for each other." Farnuk winked at Mundus, who just smiled back, giving Farnuk the least encouragement possible. Farnuk turned and clapped his greasy hands loudly. "Bring it in, boys!"

Through the large open doors of the Grand Reception room entered Chief Officer Peasly Greel and goblin deputy Wenkle Frat, both tugging behind them a large, covered trolley. Peasly and Wenkle wheezed and spluttered as they made their way across the room, pulling on the rope until the trolley came to a standstill in the center.

Farnuk gave his Chief Officer and deputy the thumbs up. "As a token of our estimated friendship, let me present to you a special gift from Tam Tower." Farnuk turned to address the whole room, to make sure that every gnome could hear his next words. "My dear gnomie brothers, let me show you the most exciting new thing since iced swampweed. This is dazzling, delirious, outright spectacular-fantastico. All behold – all *look!* – at this wondrous most excellent sight of all the realm. Da-dah!" And Farnuk whipped off the covering cloth to reveal his gigantic blob of an eye-sculpture. Everyone in the room had their eyes focused on Farnuk's monstrously ugly sculpture. A look of horror appeared on every gnome's face – a shocked expression that froze on the spot. Each and every gnome in the Grand Reception room was rooted, as if stone-gnomed. Even their expressions – their grimaces, grins, and gnome-smirks – were stuck frozen on their faces. An eerie silence descended upon the room. It became so quiet Farnuk could hear his own feverish goblin-heart pumping away in a mixture of excitement and anxiety. Slowly, Farnuk looked around the room at each gnome, seeing how each had been caught in a particular posture. Mundus had both his hands raised palm up, as if saying 'What is this?!' And Baga had his neck a little forward as if to peer closer to the eye sculpture. Fender Tart had a little smirk fixed onto his youthful gnome face as if he had had a muscle contraction.

"Did it work – are zhey stone-gnomed?" hissed Peasly in a whisper.

"They don't look like they are stone – but they're not moving." Wenkle had a confused look on his face. Farnuk didn't move, he was observing the motionless gnomes and thinking.

"Yess, yess, that's it…the human eyes still affect them, but they don't turn to stone in the Second Realm, they just freeze up. Of course, it's a different vibration here. But look at them – they can't move. Hehehehe." A wide grin erupted over Farnuk's face as he leapt into the air. "Yeaahhh – goblin-gobtastic! Yippie ay-yeah. Gotcha, you bunch of hippy beardies – hah!" Farnuk skipped around the room sticking out his tongue at all the gnomes. "Who's the goblin pappa now, eh? Who's the dude? Who's the baddest genius here, eh? Come on you fairy-loving tree-huggers – try stopping the goblin-great Farnuk Tam now!" Farnuk stuck out his tongue to the whole room and blew an almighty raspberry.

Peasly was overjoyed and couldn't stop sniggering like a manic blobfish. Wenkle was wringing his hands and nodding his head.

"You're really the most badacious sire – and you're the king now," said Wenkle as he smooched up to Farnuk.

"You bet your goblin buttocks I am! I'm the king now of the Second Realm – and I'm in gnome-busting mood. Look at me now, goblin-pappa Vernuk, I'm a gnome-busting!" Farnuk made a quick run and then slid to his knees to do a goblin slime-slide across the whole length of the floor. Peasly, caught up in the excitement of the moment, attempted to do the same but his slime-slide ended up in several tumbles and a loud bump.

"Sniper-dipers, Peasly, you trying to wake up the whole city?! We've got to get my **H**uman **E**ye **L**aunch **P**lan into Phase B. That means both you and Wenkle get yourselves down to the castle basement and release my Elite Goblin Squadron. And bring 'em here! And don't forget to put on your human eye-band," squealed Farnuk as he went and sat in Mundus's kingly wooden chair.

Peasly and Wenkle saluted before strapping on their headbands with a plastic eye in its center.

"What do yer zhink of my new zhird eye?" lisped Peasly with an inane grin.

"You're more ugly than usual, you goggled-eyed fairy-dreamer," replied Wenkle, slapping him.

"Get moving, you pair of blobfishes!" roared Farnuk from across the room. The two goblins ran out of the room, leaving Farnuk alone to admire his room of standing gnomes. He was the dude now…or so he thought.

Wenkle and Peasly scampered through the castle, looking into rooms and searching for corridors to take them to the basement below. Farnuk had been sure that this was the only place where the goblin prisoners would be kept. Along the way, Wenkle and Peasly encountered several of the castle's gnome workers. Yet all they had to do was look at them and the gnome would freeze. The goblins, wanting to be sure, would point at the human plastic eye on their forehead to every gnome they ran into. Each gnome instantly froze on seeing the three-eyed goblins. But of course, that was the whole plan. Yet the goblins didn't know that. They thought they were goblin-invincible, as goblins often do. As Wenkle and Peasly entered one corridor they saw a gnome maid walking with a bunch of sheets in her arms. They ran up to her and, as before, pointed to their third eye whilst grinning, slurping, and slavering. The gnome maid instantly froze.

"Good – now zhell us zhe way zo zhe basement," demanded Peasly. The gnome maid stood stationary, without saying a word.

"How do you expect them to speak when they are stone-gnomed, you half-brainer!"

"Well, maybe zhey can still speak when zhey are stone-gnomed?" Peasly shrugged and looked at Wenkle. It was clear that neither of them had a clue, or even a third of a clue.

"Gotta keep looking! If we don't return with the other goblins soon, Farnuk will string us up and put the itching nukk bugs all over us." Both goblins squirmed at the thought of the awful itching if they didn't complete their mission in super-quick time. They ran down another corridor, following all the open doors. It never occurred to them to wonder why it was that all the doors they arrived at were open. That is, they were just following one open door to another, since the other doors all seemed to be locked. Anyone with intelligence might think they were being led in a particular direction. But not the goblins – they were just happy to be going in *some* direction…and frantically. Once they had left the corridor the gnome maid rolled her eyes and laughed. "Those goblins are about as clever as a snotgurgle's son," she said before walking on.

Back in the Grand Reception room Farnuk was impatiently inspecting his nails and wondering where his Elite Goblin Squadron was. A plan, he knew, was all about timing. A goblin genius, such as he knew he was, had to have a decent sense of timing. It was only fair after all. Farnuk pulled himself out of Mundus's seat, which was too small for him anyway, and had another stroll around the room of motionless gnomes. "Look at you all – you're not so clever after all, are you, my little stiff gnomies?" He waved his hands about as if he were making some grand political speech. For once he had a captive audience who would listen to him without heckles, giggles, gurgles, or grunts. This occasion was not lost on Farnuk, who considered it the perfect time to launch his leadership oration. Ceremoniously he cleared his throat with a few snorts and a spit: "My fellow gnomies, and semi-respected country-folk – welcome to Tamerland. It is my grand goblin pleasure to introduce you to the new leadership of the Second Realm. Unfortunate, or rather fortunate, circumstances have put an end to the gnome rule of Grundusland. Fairy-loving gnomocracy will now be replaced by Tamtatorship – absolute rule and authority of Farnuk Tam. All tree-hugging will now be banned..." Farnuk burst into fits of sniggering. "Hehehe...banned on punishment of exile to the swamp marsh, to live amongst the bog rats, fen slime, and farkdarts!" Farnuk stamped his goblin feet in joy and leaped up and down. "You are the baddest goblin ever born under a dark star, you are Farnuk Tam – you devious slimeball you. Yesss, mister bad-tastic genius. If you were a human, you'd rule the Third Realm too! Hey...mmm." Farnuk stopped leaping around and fell into an uncharacteristic silence, with the occasional mutter and murmur as if trying to locate a running thought. He then sat down on the floor, cross-legged, and put his chin into his hands. With rolling eyes and pouting lips Farnuk went into a dangerously devious plotting mode.

Meanwhile, Wenkle and Peasly had run like blind gofers around the open corridors of Grundy Castle until, surprisingly enough, they found the stairs leading downwards. Leaping with excitement the two goblins rushed down the stairs, pushing each other out of the way, until they burst headlong into a well-lit basement. It was then that they discovered that not only was the basement well lit – it was actually far too well lit.

Veeza, the sun-deva, had illuminated the basement with her ethereal presence, shining her rays outwards like only a sun-deva can do. It was as if stepping into a golden bath of warm breezes. Wenkle and Peasly came to a braking halt and, as if paralyzed, stood rooted to the spot. They were engulfed in Veeza's rays, yet it was the most soothing sensation. The faces of the two goblins looked as if they were in goblin paradise. Their eyes were bulging as far as it was possible for eyes to bulge, which in this case meant a good thing. Their large teeth-crowded mouths were wide open, and their bat-like ears were standing up straight. For the goblins it must have felt like they were swimming in the warmest slime pools that ever existed. Yet the fact of the matter was, they were undergoing Veeza's careful hypnotic process. And this had been the plan all along. Wenkle and Peasly joined their fellows – the Elite Goblin Squadron – as recipients of Veeza's hypnotic rays of energy. The goblins were now held in a state of suspended hypnotic trance, awaiting Mundus's next move. Farnuk, of course, was still waiting impatiently for his Elite Goblin Squadron to return.

Farnuk had by this time finished his short spout of devious plotting and had returned to his oration. "The Tamtatorship of this realm is in immediate effect. I declare that all gnomes must submit to being stone-gnomed." Again, Farnuk could not stop himself from sniggering. "And all their properties shall belong to the state of Tamerland – which of course means me. Sorry, little fellas, this is no longer a gnomocracy. Oh yeah, and another thing – I'm gonna ban all those gnome-awful teas you all drink here. All that leafy stuff, yuk! I'd rather drink bog rat vomit. Really, can it be healthy, all that leafy mush in your bellies?" Farnuk was looking well pleased with himself. So pleased that he began to goblin-swagger around the room with his hands behind his back and his head held high. This meant, of course, that he didn't notice that a tiny, winged object had entered the room and flew over to where Mundus was standing.

Spritely Neem, with her wing-buzz on stealth mode, flew close to Mundus's ear to whisper her message. "Veeza says it's done. All goblins are under her hypnotic spell. You can go ahead now. I'll be watching from afar – I wouldn't miss this for anything!" Spritely gave Mundus a tiny wink and kissed him on his bearded cheek before flying up toward the ceiling.

"And another thing," continued Farnuk as he strutted about the room like a green strudel, "this is only the beginning of my most Tam-tastic plan."

"And what plan is that?"

"My plan for complete domination of all realms!" Farnuk suddenly stopped parading around the room and looked about him. Neither Peasly nor Wenkle had returned; nor any of the elite goblin squadron. "Er…who said that?"

"I did."

Farnuk scuttled around the room, looking left then right, then left again. "Who is 'I'?" called out Farnuk.

"You are Farnuk Tam – devious goblin troublemaker." A voice tittered in the room.

"No, no, not me – who are *you*?!" squealed Farnuk nervously.

"*You* are still Farnuk Tam – the rubber-belly greasy rascal."

Farnuk stomped his foot. "Nah – that's not fair! Who speaks like that to the King of Tamerland?"

"Ahem." Someone coughed.

"Well, well?"

"The King of Grundusland does." Farnuk shot a look over to where Mundus Grundy was standing. Suddenly, Mundus raised his right hand and gave a little cheeky wave. "Yo-hoo!" Mundus's bearded face erupted into a broad chuckle.

Farnuk's goggle-like eyes widened in shock, and his throat choked (or rather, croaked). Before Farnuk had chance to do anything more, all the gnomes in the room jumped up together with their hands in the air and let out an almighty cry of "YEAHHH…"

Farnuk stumbled backward and almost fell over. Instinctively, he ran to hide behind his blob of an eye sculpture. Shaking nervously, he raised his hand and, pointing at the sculpture, shouted, "Look into my eyes! Look into my eyes!" The whole room burst into a tempest of laughter.

"Your eyes are no good here!" laughed Mundus, who was having a hard time trying to compose himself.

"What?! Sniper-Dipers!" shrieked Farnuk.

"Did you really expect those plastic eyes to stone-gnome us? You're as daft as a weasel brush!"

Farnuk watched in shock as all the gnomes in the room were laughing and pointing at him. Fender was half-bent over in laughter; Baga was holding his belly and chortling away; and Rundy couldn't help but tug on his pink beard as he chuckled. Farnuk didn't like being the object of ridicule. He was Farnuk Tam, from the family of Tam – and it was his duty to ridicule others. Farnuk flew into a mighty goblin rage. He rushed out from behind the eye sculpture and waved his scaly hands at the gnomes.

"You're all doomed! I'm gonna take over all the realms – you wait and see, you fluffy-headed fairy dreamers…dahh!" And quicker than a turbo-charged ferret, Farnuk ran past all the gnomes and dashed out of the room.

Baga was first to spot the situation and went racing after Farnuk, with the other gnomes soon behind him. Yet goblins, with their rubbery long legs, are far quicker than the short-legged gnomes. Even super-athletic and fitness addict Welma Wurdy didn't have a chance in catching up with fast-legged Farnuk.

Farnuk, fueled by the rage of ridicule, steamed past the gnome guards who were meandering outside the castle door, and fled out of the city. The gnomes had not been prepared for such a radical escape and so were left huffing and puffing behind Farnuk. There was quite a bit of confusion on Nimble Street, Grundy City's main thoroughfare, as Farnuk Tam sped past the surprised gnomes, blowing out his tongue all the way.

"Next time, gnomies – next time!"

And Farnuk ran and ran, yet he wasn't heading back to Tam Tower. It wasn't just that the gnomes might follow him all the way back to his tower, or that he had no army of goblins to protect him once he got there. It was because Farnuk had been plotting another plan – which meant one destination only. Farnuk ran straight for Octagon Lodge, and for the Blue Portal. There was no gnome to stop him. With the **HOG** still etched on his arms, Farnuk jumped straight into the portal grunting the special words…and was gone.

Mundus Grundy and his armada of huffing gnomes peered into the shimmering Blue Portal in silence.

"Where's he gone to?" asked Baga. Mundus looked over at Jompa and Lompa who both shrugged.

"I reset the coordinates after the last GRALE," said Serly.

"The portal could be aligned with almost any place in the Third Realm," muttered Mundus.

"Are we going to follow?" asked an eager Fender.

Mundus shook his head. "All in good time, all in good time." He stroked his beard for a few moments, and then turned away.

The gnomes slowly sauntered back to Grundy City, where other matters awaited them.

CHAPTER NINE
GOBLIN PARADISE

Bodel Nak leaned back in the slime stone chair at the top of Tam Tower, with a large, contented grin stretched across his impish face. He knew when the goblins did not return that Farnuk's so-called Ignoble Plan had been a disaster. That was exactly his plan, and now he could implement the next phase of his takeover. Of course, there were the djinns to deal with; yet somehow, they just seemed less *physical* to Bodel. He thought this would make them less interested in Tam Tower and goblin politics.

As Bodel was plotting away in his devious head a goblin scurried into the room and stood ogling a few feet away from where the imp sat.

"Yes, what is it?" asked Bodel impatiently, as he realized this brainless goblin was not going away anytime soon.

The greasy goblin puckered his lips before speaking. "You sure you are now the new boss, right?"

"Of course I am, you impetuous imbecile. Why else would I be sitting in this chair? Do I look to you like a tourist?" Bodel sat up straight, although he still looked small in Farnuk's stone chair. Imps were, after all, fairly small creatures, and this was not lost on him. He knew immediately that he had no imp time to lose in stamping his authority over the remaining goblins in Tam Tower. "Look here, goblin —what's your name?"

"Jinker Drool," replied the goblin.

"Jinker, listen here, matey. I'm the advisor, counselor, research planner, and personal psychologist to your goblin leader Farnuk Tam. In his absence that makes me the highest-ranking dude in all of Tam Tower and the swampy lands, et cetera, et cetera. Okay? Furthermore, vis-à-vis the position of authority around here, Farnuk personally whispered to me before he left that I was to stay and take care of things in his name. Now, you can't get more proof than that! What say you, Finker?"

"It's Jinker," said the goblin without even blinking. Bodel was hoping his superior way of speaking would win the goblin over. Now he doubted if the goblin even had the intelligence to know clever words when he heard them.

"Okay, Jinker. Tell me, what do you do around here? Does Farnuk even know you exist?"

"I'm his personal cook," Jinker answered defiantly. Bodel nodded his head as if to recognize the prestige of such a position.

"Cool one, matey. And what kind of things do you cook for him?" Jinker twisted his head as if thinking.

"Well, his favorite is fried nukk bugs on a bed of mashed fenweed with a spicy frak-oil dressing."

"Mmm…well, someone likes to eat well." Bodel was impressed that Farnuk had such a tailored diet. Especially so when all the other goblins ate the usual rubbish such as bog rat stew or swamp vine soup. "Well, since you were – sorry, *are* – so close to our great leader Farnuk, I will place you as my second in command." Bodel knew that power was the greatest greed amongst the goblins. If this didn't work, nothing else would. As expected, Jinker straightened up at the news and began to slaver. "Not only will you be my deputy, but you will also be the new commander over all the remaining goblins – until Farnuk returns, of course. How many goblins are still in Tam Tower?"

"About yes, few, here and there, something…" mumbled Jinker.

"Yes, yes, Finker, whatever. Just you go and announce that you are their new commander, as my deputy. And that I'm commander-in-chief now, for the foreseeable whatever future, et cetera, et cetera."

"Jinker."

"What?"

"It's Jinker – my name is Jinker."

"Yes, yes," said Bodel with a wave of his impish hand. "Just you run along now, chappie, and do yourself a green favor." Jinker snorted in goblin delight and began hopping out of the room. "And another thing – you're *my* personal cook now. Bring me a crocodile sandwich and make it snappy!" Bodel sniggered, loving every minute of his new life. "Welcome to Nak Tower!" he said loudly, kicking up his feet as he sat on the slime stone chair.

"Don't be so sure of that," echoed a rumbling voice through a smoky whirl of mist. Bodel's impish ears pricked up as Konji materialized into a hovering column of brownish smoke, followed by the second column of Kluth.

"Hello Konji, Kluth," said Bodel trying to sound chirpy and unsurprised at their sudden appearance. He welcomed them with a smarmy look on this face.

"Behaving as if you run the tower already, little imp?" The smoky figure of Konji shifted until it was directly in front of Bodel's gaze. Bodel shifted uncomfortably in his seat.

"Look, Konji, it's like this. Someone has to rule over the remaining goblins, otherwise they would cause more chaos than they normally do. I'm just replacing the role of Farnuk and putting them in their place. It's the law of dictatorship – you replace one dictator with your own. Goblins only respond to greed and power. The goblins need someone to keep them in place. It's a simple thing really."

"And that figure of power is you, imp, is it?"

"Only because it has to be," said Bodel with a deliberately casual shrug. "The goblins, in their simple minds, need to see their leader in front of them. Seeing two columns of smoke – no offence – just wouldn't cut the cake with these green fellas. It's all psychological. Really, it's not something I actually want to do. I could be assassinated in a goblin coup any minute – but someone has to stand here and be the face of power." Bodel, of course, didn't believe a word he was saying. He knew the remaining goblins couldn't organize a slime throwing contest in a swamp. "Whereas you both, you're the power behind the scenes. It's much better to be an invisible source of power. That way nobody hassles you. You two djinns have got it easy."

"Okay, Bodel, less of the liquid verbal. You could talk yourself out of a wormhole. From now on we share power equally. You take care of the goblins, whilst Kluth and I will plan for the long-term future of this land." Bodel gulped on hearing this; the idea of a long-term djinn future didn't sound good. "Oh, and another thing – you're not calling this place Nak Tower. You're as bad as Farnuk Tam! We need a name that is more imposing."

Bodel spread his hands and gave a coy smile. He wondered just how much the djinns could actually see since they didn't seem to have faces. "Sure, no problem, it's cool. It was only a temporary name anyway. What shall we name our new home?"

"ZEROTH!" bellowed Konji. Even the smoky figure of Kluth appeared to quiver.

Over at Grundy Castle… the gnomes were left twiddling their thick-skinned thumbs. Rundy Fumbler had gone back into his gnome laboratory to continue examining goblin skin. Turdy Frump and Dundus Perky both returned to the woods to do another day's work of woodcutting and forest maintenance. Purdy Grumpus went back to doing his water maintenance and checking the streams around Grundy City. And Welma Wurdy – the greatest mud-ball thrower of all Grundusland – went back to throwing mud-balls. Fender Tart decided it was time to practice bungee jumping so he persuaded the twin brothers Jompa and Lompa to accompany him to the pimple tree forest. Baga Gheet and Serly Frundy stood five gnome-feet apart shuffling their felt boots and looking at the ground. Baga attempted to whistle, his rounded face appearing even more rounded than usual. Wobin, the plump blue cat, was purring around Serly's legs, eager for attention.

"Well, well," said Mundus as he, Baga, and Serly all stood on the main terrace of Grundy Castle. "Not such a bad outcome really."

"How do you figure that one, uncle?" Serly was not so sure about Mundus's assessment of the situation. Mundus, with his hands behind his back, strolled back and forth along the terrace.

"Well, you see, my dear niece, we gnomes have diffused the situation. We have taken the spark out of the flame, the pot off from the fire. Nothing now is going to boil over – well, not immediately anyway. We have the goblins here in the castle, all taken care of. Tam Tower has no leader, and so causes no trouble. And the only thing missing, unfortunately, is Farnuk Tam. Right now, he is no doubt hiding out somewhere in the Third Realm, keeping low and twiddling his scaly goblin fingers. So, not too bad me thinks." Baga nodded his head in agreement and attempted a casual smile over at Serly.

"Well, maybe that's so, uncle," said Serly who was still a little restless. "I still think Farnuk has some devious plans in his green head, and I don't like the idea of him being in the Third Realm. I'd rather he was being a goblin nuisance here in the Second Realm, rather than with the big fellows. For all their size, I'm not sure the big fellows would have a clue how to handle a goblin, let alone a Farnuk Tam."

Mundus pulled on his beard thoughtfully. "Mmm…you may be right, Serly. Yet first things first – let's go and visit our green guests."

Mundus, Baga, and Serly made their way to the castle basement, not quite knowing what to expect. When they arrived, they were met with an astonishing sight – all the goblins, including the elite squadron, were dancing, prancing, and cavorting around the room with huge grins on their faces. Two of the goblins looked as if they were attempting to waltz together. Another was doing a terrible disco jive with arms flailing about, whilst others were moving about the room in the most peculiar, weird ways. Mundus, Baga, and Serly didn't know what to say. They hadn't seen such a bizarre sight since old prankster gnome Pipher Noot dressed himself as a pumpkin and declared himself king of Pumpkin City!

Spritely then appeared, wearing a bright lime green jumpsuit, and whirled amongst the goblins, obviously having a lot of fun. "Wheeeee…these goblins are groovy movers and shakers!" she giggled as she flew up close to Mundus.

"I can see you are dressed to be a perfect match," said Mundus with a chuckle.

"You know me – I'm the chameleon of sprites. Now you see me, now you don't!" Spritely Neem whizzed off again and back to frolicking amongst the deliriously happy goblins.

"Veeza," called out Mundus, "can you please tell us what in gnome sense is going on here?" Almost immediately, a hazy glow appeared above the room, as if dawn had suddenly decided to arise. "Hello, Veeza, gnome greetings to you."

"And deva greetings to you, Mundus," said a soft expansive voice that seemed to fill the entire room.

"How are our friends here doing? Do they still remember our sacred **HOG**?"

"The goblins are doing very well. They are very contented. As we discussed, I have placed them all under hypnosis. They all believe they are in goblin paradise – something I thought would be a safe collective place to take their minds too. It does seem though that the goblins all share a collective mythology of paradise. This would appear, from what you can see here, to be some sort of discothèque. This could be viewed as being mildly ironic," said Veeza in her usual calm and balanced voice.

"Ironic indeed," chuckled Mundus. "Who would have thought that goblins see paradise as the ultimate disco?"

"Party time!" said Baga with a laugh.

"I think it's sweet," said Serly. "All those greasy rubber-bellied goblins want to do is get down and boogie. That's cool!"

"We have a slight situation with the Holy Oath of a Gnome, however," said Veeza. All three gnomes stopped giggling and became gnome-serious again.

"Which is?" asked Mundus.

"I have erased the memory of the **HOG** from their minds. This was not difficult since most of them had already forgotten it. The goblin mind does not operate with a subconscious, nor does it have a conscience either. A rather basic model of cerebral anatomy that operates with one preset level. That is the level of the present moment, with limited capacity for structured forward planning. The future, for goblins, is in actuality a form of present-moment desire. Goblins are motivated by the acquisition of immediate desires, which drives them forward. It is greed-motivated behavior. Only the Tam genetic line appears to have mastered a more developmental thought-structuring process. Farnuk, unlike the other goblins, has a developed cerebral brain capacity. He constantly updates his thought capability, often through forward thinking. He is evolving, and this is interesting to us."

"Mmm…and the problem with the **HOG**, Veeza?"

"Yes, Mundus, I was coming to that. As I said, the goblin brains now have no trace of the **HOG**. Where they do have a trace of it though is on their body. Each goblin has a tattoo of the **HOG**, on both of their arms. It is likely that Farnuk, knowing the goblin tendency for forgetfulness, decided a tattoo was a more favorable option than memory."

"Farnuk strikes again!" exclaimed Serly with only a slight hint of irony.

Baga beamed over at Serly. He just couldn't get over how sharp this girl gnomie was. Mundus huffed and marched over to where the goblins were still swaggering in their disco paradise. He took one of them by the elbow and looked at both arms. Sure enough, etched into the left arm were the words: heart ~ soul. And on the right arm the words – love ~ service. The goblin then grabbed Mundus by both arms and tried to swing him around in a rock 'n' roll jive.

"Get offa me! You ain't nothing but a hound-goblin!" Even Baga and Serly had to laugh, coyly looking at each other. Spritely whizzed over Mundus's head as he struggled to break away from the boogying goblin.

"Jive on, you rocking gnome muffin!" shouted out Baga.

"Smecker!"

*****

Later that same day, Baga and Serly paid a visit to Churly's Teahouse on Nocker Lane. Churly had by now become accustomed to seeing the chubby blue cat in the establishment. She had, in this case, allowed an exception. She made it clear, however, that one exception does not lead to another. And if any other gnome was planning on bringing back any furry critters from the Third Realm, they had better keep them away from Churly's Teahouse. As Churly had said aloud on more than one occasion, "Nocker Lane is no place for four-legged fluff-balls in need of yoga!" Ironic, considering Churly was the gnome equivalent of a steak and cheeseburger pie.

Serly and Baga were seated at what they now considered to be *their* table, as they sat there every time they came for tea and chats – which was now becoming something of a habit.

"So, what did Mundus and Veeza finally decide to do?"

"About the goblins?"

"Yes, and the **HOG**," asked Serly.

Baga smiled into his nettle tea. "Well, they were sent home of course. Grundy City is no place for boogying goblins."

Serly laughed at this and gave Baga a playful poke. "You smecker, Baga – I can't believe you called my uncle a rocking gnome muffin!" Both Serly and Baga broke into fits of giggles. "But really, what's going to happen to them?"

"Well, Veeza says the hypnotic trance will wear off once they're back in Tam Tower."

"And what about the **HOG** that's tattooed onto their arms?"

"Ah, now that's a different matter. There was not much that could be done. Veeza couldn't un-do the tattoo."

"So?"

"So, Mundus decided on something different," said Baga as he leaned over and, pulling away her blonde locks, whispered into her ear. Serly put her hand over her mouth to suppress her giggling.

"Ohh, that's sooo bad – the poor old goblins!" At that moment, Lompa came dashing into the teahouse and, looking around, saw Baga and Serly. He ran up to them panting.

"Looking for you, Baga, thought you might be here. You gotta come quickly."

"What's up, Lompa?"

"It's Fender Tart – he's gone and hurt himself!"

"What! How?"

"Bungee jumping from a pimple tree!"

Lompa, followed by Baga and Serly, ran at top gnome speed towards Grundusland Forest where the pimple trees grew. Wobin, the chubby blue shorthair cat, ran alongside Serly, not wanting to leave her side. When they arrived in the forest, they saw Fender hanging upside down about two meters from the ground, attached to a tall pimple tree.

Around his ankles was tied a large band of vine that was tied at the other end to a branch of the pimple tree. Fender wasn't moving or making a sound, which was indeed unusual for him.

"What the gnome is going on?" asked Baga to the stony silent Lompa and Jompa. The gnome twins looked at each other, each mirroring the other's puzzled expression.

"I don't think he's gnome conscious," said Jompa finally. Baga's and Serly's jaws both dropped open.

"Holy Gnomey!" gasped Serly. "We need to get Dr. Dundus immediately. Lompa, can you fetch him?" Lompa nodded and sped off at haste, followed by his brother, Jompa. They ran together, side by side, as if their feet were tied together in a three-legged race.

Baga scrambled up the tree to the branch where the vine was tied. "Damn it," he said with a huff. "It's a merkle tree vine he used."

"And so?"

"It's an elastic vine that doesn't have an elastic limit, so it can keep on stretching. We used to use it in the mines for quick vertical deliveries. Fender should have known this – unless he had pixie-fluff on his brain. Here, catch him as I cut his feet loose." Serly stood beneath Fender, waiting for the drop. Fender fell into her arms, and they crashed to the ground. Yet gnomes are hardy creatures – it takes a lot to make a dent in a gnome.

"Poor Fender," said Serly as she nestled his head in her arms. "His little gnomie head would have hit the ground. You're such a wild thing."

Serly was then surprised to see Fender open one of his eyes, pucker-up his lips as if for a kiss, and then with a grin he whispered, "You make my heart sing."

"Smecker!!"

Baga huffed and huffed and huffed a little more.

CHAPTER TEN
INSURRECTION AT TAM TOWER

The Goblin Elite Squadron, deputy Wenkle Frat, and Chief Officer Peasly Greel all tromped back to Tam Tower like marching automatons. Jinker Drool, after hopping frantically around the tower, finally found Bodel rummaging in Farnuk's private quarters. Jinker was as surprised as he was frantic.

"What you doing in Farnuk's rooms? They not for you!"

"Ah, my dear fellow, I am here because of you," replied Bodel unfazed.

"Yes?" Jinker's face didn't know which expression to make, like drippy wax that doesn't yet have a final shape.

"Of course, you would not have found me here otherwise. Now, how can I help?"

Jinker fumbled for his words, waving his arms excitedly. "The other goblins are back. They're all coming in now!"

"Eeek!" Bodel couldn't hide his shock at the news. This was not what he was expecting. "All of them are coming back – ALL of them?"

Jinker nodded. "Yess, the goblin squadron, and Chief Officer Peasly. I seen 'em myself. And Wenkle too – they just come marching back. They're standing outside in the courtyard, and they ain't said a word."

"Mmmm…and our good goblin leader Farnuk – has he come back too?" Bodel was becoming very nervous at the thought. He had well-laid plans, and Farnuk was not a part of them.

Jinker's face strained, and his lips pouted. "Nope, nope, can't say that he has, or I ain't seen him," he said with a shake of his head.

"Good. So, you're still commander of the other goblins here whilst I'm commander-in-chief. Now go and bring the other goblins up here into the tower and lock the doors to the courtyard. And do it goblin speed quick!" Bodel almost pushed Jinker out the door before he could think of any reply. This was not good news for Bodel. Running to the top of the tower, Bodel called out for the djinns. It was time to consolidate power.

Meanwhile, a spewd of trance-like goblins were standing below in the courtyard of Tam Tower (that is, Zeroth Tower). At first, they just stood there, as if rooted to the spot. Then slowly, one after the other, they each began to shake their heads as if arousing from some deep slumber. The look of surprise on their faces was obvious, as they each peered around the courtyard slowly. Chief Officer Peasly waggled over to where Wenkle Frat was standing, goggle-eyed.

"Where is zhe disco, Wenkle?"

Wenkle pouted with a look of sadness and shook his head. "Disco days over," he mumbled. "We're back home. No more of the boogie." Wenkle wobbled a little unsteady on his feet as he moved around the courtyard, pushing through the similarly disorientated elite squadron. "Where's Farnuk?" Peasly shrugged and flapped his arms in the air. "Hey, what's that on your arms, Peasly? You got some markings."

"What you zhalking about, you rubber weasel?"

Wenkle went over to Peasly and grabbed his arms. Etched into Peasly's left arm were the words: heartless ~ soulless. And on the right arm the words: loveless ~ servitude.

"What you gone got tattooed like that for, Peasly?"

Peasly scowled, then grabbed Wenkle's arms. "You got zhe same, you stinky-finger!"

Wenkle looked down at his arms. "Gobly gooks! What in the name of swamp sickness is that?" Wenkle hopped over to where the elite squadron were milling around in a brainless daze and began checking all their arms. "They've all got them, Peasly!" he called back. "We all got these words stamped on our arms." Peasly got excited and began hopping from one foot to the other. "What you so pleased about, Peasly?"

"We're zhe elite of zhe elite goblins now! We're zhe chosen ones, Wenkle. Don't you see it? We've been marked for goblin greatness!" Peasly was beaming.

Slowly a wide grin erupted over Wenkle's face, and he leapt in the air with a goblin high kick. "Ye-ha! We're goblin-tastic! We've been upgraded."

"Yeah, yeah – we were in goblin paradise. You saw it zhoo, didn't you Wenkle?"

"Sure did, Peasly, my goblin buddy. We were taken to paradise to show us a taste of what is to come if we do goblin good. Or rather," sniggered Wenkle, "if we do goblin badness. The almighty Stinky-Finger himself has marked us as his servants. Look – our arms – we are in servitude to the Almighty Goblin One!" Wenkle was wringing his hands and slavering.

"And Farnuk?"

"Farnuk isn't here, is he? Looks as if the Almighty Goblin One didn't elect him. It is our goblin elite-elite duty to do what the Almighty asks. And he asks through us, doesn't he?"

Peasly grinned and nodded.

Wenkle turned to the spewd of goblins still lingering in the courtyard. "Oh, hear me, gather round chosen goblins. This is a new day in goblinstory." The spewd shuffled around Wenkle, who was now bloating out his rubber-belly and smirking excitedly. Peasly stood beside him, nodding his head. "We who stand here today are the chosen goblin elite. If you do not believe me, look at your arms. We are imprinted with the mark of the Almighty Goblin One. We have been marked out to worship and serve the Almighty Stinky-Finger. This day marks the beginning of a new goblinosophy. It is a revolution – it is time for a goblin republic! Down with the goblin rule of the Tam clan – we have no goblin ruler but the Almighty Stinky-Finger! Our day is at hand – rise goblin masses and follow me as Chief Goblin Priest!" Wenkle had built up to a climax and was now shrieking at the top of his voice. All the goblins of the former Elite Goblin Squadron cheered – as they didn't know what else to do, or they probably just didn't understand.

Peasly leaned over and whispered to Wenkle. "What is zhe name of zhis new goblinosophy?"

"Ahem…yes. As Chief Goblin Priest of this new republic, and with Peasly as Deputy Priest, I announce the arrival of *Goblinism*!"

"Goblinism?"

Wenkle looked at Peasly and shrugged. "It's an *ism*, isn't it?"

"You could have gone for an *ology*?" suggested Peasly.

Bodel was looking down on the courtyard scene from the top window of the tower. "What the blinkers are those goblins up to?" The smoky figure of the djinn Konji was moving around the room.

"It is something unexpected, is it not, imp Bodel?" Bodel ignored the patronizing tone of Konji's voice.

"It is a damn inconvenience, yes. Goblins can never be trusted, even to do things wrong. So, what's our next move?"

"Our?" Konji's voice seemed to groan around the room as if in stereo-sound.

"Yes, of course, Konji. We are equal collaborators in this venture of ours." A low sound, something like a cross between a titter and a grunt, echoed in the room and made Bodel shiver. At that instance, a second smoky form materialized in the middle of the tower room.

"It doesn't look good," moaned Kluth.

"Huh. Sometimes, Kluth, I don't know if you're talking or complaining. Or maybe there isn't a difference?" boomed Konji.

"There is a difference, dear – if you care to listen."

"What was that?"

"Nothing, my dear. I only said, would you care to listen?"

"Yes, we would," burst in Bodel. He wanted to hear the news before the djinns got into a domestic tussle.

"Well, it doesn't look good. It seems like the goblins are starting some sort of revolution. They are now downstairs trying to break through the main door. The cook and several other incompetent goblins are panicking and scurrying around like…well, like…scurrying goblins really."

"Ever the imaginative one," sighed Konji.

Bodel stamped his foot. "Oh imp-shrimps! What are we going to do?!"

"Get the goblin cook to bake a revolution strudel," moaned Konji sarcastically.

Down in the courtyard, Wenkle was directing his new elite Goblinism Guard in trying to break into Tam Tower. The main door, however, was made extra secure by the Tam clan for this very reason.

"It's not breaking," hissed Peasly.

Wenkle wrung his hands and peered up the sides of the tower. "The new Goblinism Guard must be tested. We must test their faith." He ordered the goblin guard to scale the sides of the tower. When they all looked at him blankly, he called out – "Climb with your new goblin faith, brothers!"

The next few minutes saw goblin after goblin attempt to scramble up the slimy sides of the tower. And each time, they fell down in a greasy heap at the base.

"It's zhoo slimy, Wenkle."

"Not enough faith, Peasly. Anyway, we can help their faith with something. As ex-Chief Officer, what do we have for moments like this?"

Peasly scratched his green expressionless face. "We have climbing rope and hooks, for when we used zho go rock climbing."

Wenkle slapped Peasly on the back. "Brilliant, Peasly – your faith is strong. Go and command our faithful."

Peasly hopped off and before long he was back with coils of rope and hooks.

Bodel came running down the tower stairs like a crazier than crazy imp. "Finker, where are you?!"

The cook Jinker Drool was sitting on a stool in the tower kitchens looking despondent. "It's Jinker," he said as Bodel rushed up to him.

"Yes, yes, but what are you doing?"

"Sitting in my kitchen."

Bodel slapped his little imp hand against his own head. "You're the commander – you've got to do something!"

"Like what?"

Bodel didn't respond immediately but hopped around the kitchen, opening cupboards and drawers. "What's in all these jars? What's this green liquid?"

Jinker peered over to where Bodel was ferreting around in one of the kitchen cupboards. "That's swamp weed oil. I use it in my cooking; and for soups."

"Swamp weed oil – so, it's an oil?" Bodel popped off one of the tops and stuck his fingers in. "Erggh, greasier than bog rat snot – great!"

"What's so great about that?" Jinker shrugged and made a long goblin face.

"It's great because you and the other goblins are going to take this snot juice and pour it from every window in the tower. I want all the outer walls covered in this slime oil – got it?"

"And then what?" sneered Jinker.

Bodel paused for thought. "Then I make you supreme commander of all goblins." Jinker leapt up and started to cram the bottles into his arms.

Back in the courtyard, the elite Goblinism Guard was still trying to throw the ropes and their hooks up and through the lower windows. Yet they didn't seem to be having much luck.

"I thought the goblins were trained in this, Peasly?"

"Zhey are out of practice. Or maybe it's zhe shock of being chosen by zhe Almighty Goblin One?"

Wenkle frowned and gave Peasly a long, hard stare. Then suddenly, the first hook was through a window and a goblin began to climb. Soon after, other goblins managed to get their hooks through and were climbing too – slowly and unsteady at first.

"This is a groovy sight," said a now delighted Wenkle. "A great occasion for the goblin revolution." Wenkle's pleasure was short lived for as soon as he had spoken a green liquid was poured from the tower windows. Each of the climbing goblins began slipping on the walls, hanging like green snotdrops, until every one of them fell and landed, once again, in a greasy heap at the bottom.

"Dah! What's going on in that tower – don't they want to be saved?"

"I guess revolutions aren't easy," said Peasly with a shrug.

"We should not lose faith, brother – our time is at hand. Farnuk's sacrifice has ended the old Tam dynasty. The times, deputy priest Peasly, are a-changing."

"Yess, Chief Priest Wenkle. Goblinism is zhe new green. Why zhink small when we can zhink big?"

"Yes, brother – deep words indeed. Yet why think big when we can think huge?" Wenkle and Peasly started sniggering together as the new Goblinism Guard lay crumpled on the floor nearby.

Bodel was peering down from the kitchen window, high up in the tower. He knew he had delayed the advance – but for how long? "What's up with Wenkle and Peasly?" he muttered to himself.

"Goblin-knows!"

Bodel quickly turned around and saw Jinker fiddling with some pots and pans. He had almost forgotten about the goblin cook.

"Cooking up another plan?" Bodel said half-sarcastically.

Jinker shook his head. "Nope. Me, I'm a cook, so cooking up some sprog balls in rat fat – want some?"

Bodel winced. He never could appreciate goblin cuisine. Well, he couldn't even call it cuisine. "Nah, not for me. I've got enough goblin problems to worry about. Maybe one day I'll give you a recipe for brains." Bodel grinned as he scuttled out of the kitchen in search of the djinns.

"Brains? Mmmm…"

Wenkle and Peasly were still sniggering when a smoky figure materialized and coughed a 'ahem' behind them. Both goblins nearly jumped out of their green slimy skins.

"What! What the…?!"

"Brothers, be calm. It is your friend and ally, Kluth."

"Ah, Kluth," said Wenkle with a goblin grin. He eyed the smoky apparition suspiciously. "Are you not with that impy fellow – what's his name?"

"You refer to Bodel Nak, the imp. We, the djinns, were aiding Farnuk and yourselves. We assumed the imp was doing the same. Our obligation was, and still is, to the goblins. What the imp Bodel is up to we cannot say. He seems to have gone a little – well, a little unstable. Yet the djinns are here to support your revolution, brothers!" The low hypnotic moan of Kluth filled the air around Wenkle and Peasly.

"You support the revolution? And the faith of Goblinism?" Wenkle and Peasly both looked surprised at Kluth's revelation.

"We djinns support the goblins, and your right to rule – we always have. Now, we have some small suggestion for you…if you care to listen."

Two smoky figures hovered in the distance as they watched a spewd of goblins trying to climb onto each other's shoulders to make a chain.

"So, they believed you then?"

"Yes, my dear. I said exactly what you told me to say," groaned Kluth.

"Good. Then this whole affair will soon be sorted. The goblins are so tiresome. Really, revolution in the name of faith today – what tomorrow?"

"Yes, my dear, you're quite right."

"Now for the imp. Come." Konji's smoky form dissolved into nothingness, as did Kluth.

The smell of fatty sprog balls wafted through the tower making the air feel greasy. Bodel, alone in the top tower room, was peering out the window onto the scene below. The goblins were making a ladder of themselves against the wall, with each goblin climbing onto the shoulders of the one below. Bodel reckoned that in about two more goblins they would reach the first window – then they would be inside.

"Finker! Finker!" Bodel, now panicking, scampered back down the tower stairs and toward the kitchen. "Finker, where's my goblins?!" Bodel almost slipped as he came rushing into the kitchen.

"It's Jinker," said the goblin cook as he scooped out another portion of fried sprog balls onto a plate.

Bodel's eyes widened in dismay as he looked around the kitchen and saw that it was full of goblins, all slurping away on bowls of sprog balls. A thick greasiness hung in the air. He gulped.

"Jinker, we need all the goblins protecting the windows – now! It's critical!" Bodel jumped up and down in front of the cook, as if trying to impress the urgency of the situation.

"I don't know what is critical. That sounds like an imp word to me. But I know we goblins are hungry. Nothing happens here 'til we fill our bellies. Next!"

Bodel heard a loud thud followed by two smaller ones, which sounded like a body hitting the floor and then bouncing. And next he heard the sound of hopping, and then the creak of the front door as the latch was taken off and then opened. Bodel shivered as he knew the spewd of goblins were about to enter the tower. He ran at super-fast imp-speed to the top tower room. He was relieved when he saw two smoky forms quivering in the center of the room when he arrived.

"Konji, Kluth – we've been infiltrated!"

"Mmm…doesn't look good, does it, Bodel?"

"Okay, Konji, less of the obvious. What we need now is evasive action. Got it?"

"Got it." The two smoky figures immediately disappeared. After about 30 seconds, Bodel realized that this invasive action plan didn't involve him.

"Okay, okay. Haha, the djinns have a sense of humor. I salute you," called out Bodel, who was now starting to grovel slightly. "All right, let's talk about this. We're all rational beings here."

A few moments later the familiar sight of a smoky, hazy figure appeared.

"Bodel, this is Kluth. It seems like you're in a bit of a bind here. Maybe I can help you out?"

"Well, let's say I'm in a situation here, Kluth. Okay, what do you suggest?"

"You cannot leave through the front door; there's no back door; and it's too high to jump. And, of course, where would you go?" Bodel scratched his chin as if considering the implications.

"Mmm, yes – there are these considerations. Yet once I'm out of here I could go to the Third Realm. I could still use the **HOG,** which we got from that gnome."

"And do you remember the **HOG**?"

Bodel thought he heard a low chuckle coming from the smoky figure. He tried to think…what was it that the gnome had said under hypnosis? "Eeek, damn it!" he squealed.

"That's right. No matter how hard you try, you'll not be able to remember the **HOG**. Only the gnomes can remember it permanently."

Bodel stamped his foot on the floor in frustration. "Okay then – so what do you propose?"

"Come with me. I will take you. Step into me and we can leave here now."

Bodel hesitated. He then heard the sound of many flat feet hopping up the tower stairs. He knew his time was running out. With a sigh of trepidation, he stepped forward into the smoky haze.

Wenkle Frat, followed by Peasly Greel and the elite Goblinism Guard, burst into the kitchen. Wenkle was now wearing a red piece of cloth that he had picked up somewhere along the way. Tied around his neck and nearly touching the floor it looked almost like a robe. All the goblins seated at the large kitchen table looked up, then returned to slurping their food.

"I, Wenkle Frat, as Chief Goblin Priest, declare the new goblin republic under the authority of *Goblinism*! And with Peasly here as Deputy Priest, I announce that Tam Tower is now under the authority of the Almighty Stinky-Finger. We hereby rename this tower as Revolution Tower. As the representatives of the Almighty Stinky-Finger, Peasly and I will govern the New Goblin Republic. This shall be a new dawn for goblinism! All those who wish to join the revolution and the new republic raise your goblin arms." All the goblins in the kitchen raised one of their arms without looking up and carried on licking their bowls. "Right on – keep the faith, brothers!" shouted Wenkle as he shot his fist into the air. He then turned and left the kitchen to continue his inspection of the new Revolution Tower, with Peasly following behind. By the time they reached the top of the tower all they found was an empty room.

"The faithless one has flown," muttered Wenkle.

"Impy bye-bye," snorted Peasly.

Wenkle went and sat in the slimy stone chair that had once belonged to Farnuk Tam. "This is our new dawn, Peasly. We are in servitude to the Almighty Stinky-Finger – nothing's gonna stop us now!"

Somewhere else... Bodel opened his eyes and looked around. He couldn't see very far or make out any object as it was all very misty. It was like standing in the middle of a swamp fog, without any sense of direction.

"Hello?" he called out meekly.

"Bodel. Good to have you with us." The low voice of Konji almost sounded sarcastic.

"Ah, Konji. Where am I?"

"You are with us, Bodel. You are ours now, little imp. You work for us – we own you!"

Bodel could hear the thundering laugh of both Konji and Kluth bellowing around him as a distorted echo. He gulped nervously.

CHAPTER ELEVEN
STRANGE GOBLIN IN A STRANGE LAND

The dark night sky shivered with stars blinking in and out. The only creatures stirring were those that navigated the darkness other than by human sight. Grey foxes were prowling, squirrels were skulking, cougars were crouching, the odd black bear was sniffing the wind, and…someone, or something, was plod hopping. Along a deserted country road, a small, spindly figure was flat-feet hopping along and hiss-whistling. Hiss-whistling is what goblins do to pass the time – it's a bit like singing, but without a melody, words, rhythm, or tune. To a person with an untrained ear, it would sound something like air being released from a bicycle tire. Yet for Farnuk Tam, it was the hiss-whistling of someone on a mission. First things being first, Farnuk was searching for a place to chill-out and rest his rubbery flat feet. All he needed was the right place, and perhaps the right person to meet. He was sure he had the right time. Farnuk felt assured that now it was *his* time. Why else would goblin-destiny have ensured his rapid move out of the Second Realm?

Farnuk saw on his left a small lane with a large iron-bar gate. This was a good sign: where there are gates, there are things to protect. And where there are things to protect, there are always people who have fear about losing things. And people who have fear are the exact type of people Farnuk was looking for. Fear attracts goblins, which then attracts devious plans for greed. It was a wonderful chain of connections that made him grin an almighty deviously delicious goblin grin.

Farnuk slipped through the iron-bar gate and plod-hopped down the lane. In the distance, against the first haze of dawn, was silhouetted the outline of a large house. He decided that he should do a goblin search of the place. But first he had other priorities, which meant that every goblin genius needed his sleep. And thinking that, he slipped into the first shelter he came to, which was a short distance away from the house.

Farnuk yawned and stretched his arms wide. "Argghh, another day in this miserable realm of giant blob-fishes!" he moaned as he sat up and looked around. The place was a far cry from Tam Tower. Gone were the slimy stone walls; now replaced with wooden beams and four-legged creatures. Four-legged creatures? Farnuk opened his eyes even wider. He didn't know it yet, but he had just spent a few hours sleeping in a barn. It was a warm place, and stinking of horse manure – in fact, an almost ideal place for a goblin to be taking temporary residence. One of the two horses in the barn whinnied and shuffled its feet. "Oh, stop your bellyaching, you four-legged overgrown ferret!" snapped Farnuk as he sprung up onto his flat feet. "Now, what to do today to start with the Great Farnuk Plan. Yess, I'll have those bearded tree-huggers begging at my feet before long. Damn those fluff-ball do-gooders…erghh…makes me shiver just thinking of them." Suddenly, the sound of the barn door creaked open, and a pair of dark boots walked in. Farnuk scuttled behind one of the stalls as he watched a small figure enter the barn and begin to fiddle with some things. Farnuk watched closely.

"It's not fair. I shouldn't be the one doing this. I must have loads of likes and messages waiting for me on my Influencer page." Farnuk listened as the small person talked to himself, which seemed to him to be similar to the horse's whining. Farnuk, ever the opportunist, was willing to take a risk. He glanced around, and seeing what looked like a rubber ball, he picked it up and rolled it out across the floor to where the small person was doing his things. The figure in the dark boots turned around and kicked the ball back. Farnuk grabbed the ball and rolled it back. Once again, it was kicked back, and again Farnuk rolled it back.

"Hey, who's there?" called out a high-pitched young voice. "Come out, whoever you are – this is private property!" Farnuk noticed there was a tone of unease and nervousness in the voice – just what he needed! Farnuk popped his head around the stall and peered over at the young person in the dark boots.

"Ahhh!" shrieked the figure as it jumped back. Farnuk hid behind the wooden stall again, then slowly reappeared. He saw a look of shock and surprise on the young fellow's face. Farnuk grinned and could not resist a goblin wave.

"It's…it's ET!" stammered the young fellow.

"Stop it – you're freaking me out!" snapped Farnuk, who had now appeared fully in front of the small fellow.

"What…what do you want?" the young fellow continued to stammer.

Farnuk tilted his head and thought for a while. "How about I eat your brain?"

"Ahhh!"

"Only kidding! Calm down – I'm sure it would be too mushy anyway. So, you're a little human, right?"

"What…er…what do you mean?"

"What I mean is what you are, right?" said Farnuk pointing at the shaking figure.

"I'm a boy. A human…yes, a huu-man," said the boy in slow syllables.

"Yes, yes, I'm not an illiterate imp!" Farnuk snorted as he hopped over to where the boy was standing. The boy backed away nervously.

"Did…did you l-l-lose y-your ship?" he stammered. "Do you want…to…p-h-o-n-e…h-o-m-e?" The last words were said with a special, deliberate emphasis.

"Sniper-dipers! What do I look like boy, a Cabbage Patch doll missing its mother? I'm here for realm domination – for messing with your minds! Where did *you* come from – the local refuse swamp?"

The boy stood up straight and regained some composure. "Hey, watch what you say. I live here; this is my house. And you are trespassing."

"Tres-what? The only thing I'm passing here is my precious time," grunted Farnuk.

"So, you're not an alien?" Farnuk sniffed the boy's dark boots, and then tried to take a bite. "Heyy! Get off! What are you doing, you little rat-thing!"

Farnuk leapt onto the back of the boy and jumped up until he was sitting on his shoulders. With his greasy goblin legs hanging around the neck, he placed both scaly hands over the boy's eyes.

"Listen here, snot-boy. I am Farnuk Tam, the leader of all the goblins. You're the rat-thing, and I'm the goblin genius. Got it?" The boy vigorously shook his head. "You got a name, or shall I give you one?"

"Randy. Randy Travis," the boy replied.

"Mmm…sounds like a punishment. Randy…Raanndy – is that really a boy's name, or is it an excuse for something else?"

"Hey, stop it. That's my name! And my family is very rich and quite important, so watch what you're saying. I could have you arrested. Besides, you shouldn't exist – there are no goblins here."

"That's right, Randy old boy. There are no goblins here, until now! Welcome to *my* world – the world of Tam." Farnuk leapt off the boy and hopped over to the door. "So, that's your house up there, the big one?"

"Yes. Well, it's my parents' house, but mine too I guess." But Farnuk wasn't really listening, he was staring at the house and too engrossed in his own thoughts. Randy continued to speak. "You're the only goblin here in the world – and you're in my house?"

"What? Ergh, yeah, Randy, that's what I said. You people in the Third Realm don't believe in us. You got your colored boxes to make your beliefs. But we goblins are as real as swamp slime, bograts, and farkdarts. And your world needs a bit of Farnuk Tam."

Randy walked over to Farnuk and bent down to stare at him. Farnuk glared back at the pale face of the boy, beneath a mop of light blondish hair.

"What you looking at, ghost-boy? You woken up yet from your human sleep? Yess…I-am-real – got it? Now stop freaking me out. So, tell me, how many human years do you have?'

Randy backed away and thought for a moment. 'I have thirteen human years, as you say,' he replied as he stood up straight. Randy was thin and quite tall for his age. Although his face was young it showed a determined look, which was exaggerated by a thin, bony nose.

"Me and you, Randy ghost-boy – we can do good things together." Farnuk grinned wide and winked at the boy.

Randy grinned back. "Yeah, I'm beginning to think that we can," he whispered quietly. "Yes, this could be a good thing after all. A real-live ET goblin, and he's here."

Farnuk's bat-like ears sprung up; he was sensing some devious vibes coming his way. He had a feeling that Randy was going to work out just fine for his plans.

"Randy, matey, we're unique, you and me. I'm the only goblin in your realm. And I also happen to be Farnuk Tam, the goblin genius and ruler back in my realm. So, that makes me like a goblin king. And I'm here to make friends with important people – boy-kings – because I have power. I have a feeling that you and me, Randy, we can go far together. Fancy a bit of power?"

Randy's eyes lit up. "Oh yeah, sure thing! I was born for power – I'm a Travis. We're born to rule, that's what my daddy says."

"Yess…daddy's so right, Randy boy." Farnuk stuck out his scaly claw-like hand. "So, we got a deal then? We two work together – you and me, Randy – and we'll rule this realm together?"

"We will?"

"One day, snot-boy – one day soon!" Randy stuck out his hand and shook with Farnuk.

"Great, now make me a swamp weed sandwich. I'm starving!"

It didn't take Farnuk long to get himself exactly where he wanted to be. Farnuk moved into Randy's wing of the house, unbeknown to the rest of the Travis family. Here, between the large bedroom, the study room, and the playroom, Farnuk was once again king of himself. Randy spent all of his spare time with his new partner, showing Farnuk the Internet and how to surf and use emails.

"This is swamp slime cool! This internet thingy-giggy – it's the nukk knees of deceitfulness. It's the bestest thing since fenweed got mashed! You humans are more deviously dafty than we thought."

Randy grinned and took it as a compliment. "Yeah, cool, ain't it? I can communicate with all my mates – and my girlfriends. And all hours of the day – even when I should be sleeping."

"You can forget your mates, Randy ol' boy, and those girl-whatevers. You got the minds of your realm plugged into this invisible swamp net. All these machiney-thingys you have in your homes. All you big fellows are tied into the wobbly energy grid like bograts, and you don't know it. You dafter-than-dumb geniuses – you're goblin-tastic!" Farnuk leapt about the rooms displaying a new frenetic energy.

"So, you're not going home in your ship anytime soon?"

"Stop freaking me, boy! Do you think I'm a fairy-loving gofer? No, Randy, this Tam is staying here. It's gonna be sooo much fun! Right, another plate of those raw onion thingys – I'm still starving."

Farnuk sat back on the chair's cushion with an almighty grin. Things were looking up for the Tam goblin dynasty.

CHAPTER TWELVE
THE HARMONY OF THE THREE REALMS

Mundus Grundy was taking a kingly stroll down Nimble Street, observing life on Grundy City's main thoroughfare. All around him gnomes were going about their daily business; never rushing. It seemed that strolling was what gnomes did a lot of when they had free time on their hands – other than drinking tea. Mundus, in his purple felt hat, was nodded at and greeted by the other gnomes as they passed by. It was not unusual for the King of Grundusland to take a gentle leisurely meander through the city streets and to chat with the city folk. Or, for that matter, to ramble through the fields or to call on those neo-primitive gnomes who were living off gnome-grid in their wooden cabins. A gnome was a gnome was a gnome: Mundus respected them all, and they all respected Mundus in return. It was, to be fair, a relatively stable form of gnomocracy.

Mundus was lost in thought, thinking about the recent events with the goblins, when he ran into his gnome buddies Turdy Frump and Dundus Perky. Both Turdy and Dundus were woodsman and had grown up with Mundus. They were old friends who had shared many a countryside clean-up together.

"Hey, Mundus!" called out Turdy and Dundus together as they passed with bundles of firewood on their backs.

Mundus smiled and waved back. Friendly as he was, Mundus was not in the mood for a gnome-buddy chat right at that moment. He was preoccupied with what Farnuk Tam might be up to. Mundus knew that he had escaped somewhere into the Third Realm; and knowing Farnuk, he would be making the best of the situation. Mundus was thinking about what Veeza had said earlier about Farnuk, and it was now troubling him. Veeza had said that the Tam line of goblins had displayed a different form of cerebral activity. That is, their brains had showed an unusual form of developmental capacity. In the case of Farnuk Tam, Veeza had explicitly said that he was evolving. And an evolving goblin hiding out in the Third Realm was not a good thing. No, it certainly was not a good thing at all. And what was also not a good thing, as far as Mundus was concerned, were the recent erratic energy patterns occurring in the Third Realm. It was as if something was affecting the energy matrix, and the environment had been going loopy because of it. A lot of work for the gnomes, to be sure – yet there had to be more to it.

In his pensive mood, Mundus carried on his amble through the city's streets. It always lifted his humor to be amongst fellow gnomes. A gnome's good disposition was an infectious energy. Mundus walked in the direction of Nobblers Avenue, the popular and trendy area of Grundy City where all the gnome fashion shops were located. Here, gnomes young and old were mingling, excitedly looking into the shop windows, or trying on the latest fashion-colored waistcoat or dress. As Mundus passed what was the trendiest, most hip shop on Nobblers Avenue – Marty Furly's Fashion House – he could not resist a quick peek through the window. "Gnome me!" mumbled Mundus to himself. "If it isn't old Rundy Fumbler himself. What the gnome-beard is he up to in there?" Mundus stepped inside the shop with a huge grin on his face.

"Hello there, Rundy! What's a gnome scientist and inventor doing in a shop like this? No offence, Marty."

"None taken, Mundus," said a dandy looking young gnome. Marty Furly, the owner of the shop, was one top fashion-conscious gnome. A young male (just turned 301 gnome years), he wore a multi-colored striped felt hat with matching waistcoat, and his beard slicked thin with bristle gel. "You're just so on time to be here now, Mundus; I have just the thing for you," said Marty as he skipped into the back room.

Mundus shook his head and turned back to Rundy, who was coyly trying to avoid Mundus's gaze. "Hey, Rundy, you going to be our first fashion scientist?" He chuckled.

"Mundus, it's not like that," replied Rundy, somewhat embarrassed. "I'm, err, just, you know, checking things out. Got to keep on top of things."

Marty came dashing back into the shop. "Ohh, Mundus, what kingly new trousers I have for you." He held up a pair of bright yellow trousers with a pink strip running down the outside leg.

Mundus cocked his head to one side as if considering the new look. "Mmm…no thank you, Marty. I don't think the colors are quite me yet."

Marty obviously thought differently yet didn't wish to contradict the king. "Well, next season then, Mundus. We at Marty Furly's Fashion House will make sure our king is gnome-hip." Marty smiled and then looked over at Rundy who was still standing around. "Okay, Rundy, back to you. Now, we were looking for some pink for you to match your new fashion beard."

Mundus, trying very hard to suppress a giggle, nodded quickly to them both and left the shop. As he did so he almost ran into Fender Tart with Lompa and Jompa, who were walking quickly down the avenue.

"Whoah!" Mundus swerved quickly to avoid a collision.

"Sorry, Mundus, cannot stop," called back Fender. "Got to collect some herb scents!"

Lompa and Jompa gave a typical expressionless half-wave greeting. What in Grundusland does young Fender want with herb scent? wondered Mundus. It seemed as if young Fender was getting odder by the day. He was either in love or had a trick up his gnome-sleeve, thought Mundus. He hoped he was not going to become another crazy Pipher Noot!

Mundus left Nobblers Avenue and turned into Needit Street, where the city's DIY, tool shops, and bric-a-brac shops were located. The locals generally referred to it as 'useful street.' Mundus noticed Purdy Grumpus, his other gnome buddy, who was responsible for the water maintenance in Grundy City. Purdy was coming out of a shop with tubes hanging off his shoulders, and his regular toolkit bag strapped to his belt at the waist.

"Hello, Mundus, fine day for plugging leaks," said Purdy as he happily walked by. Mundus greeted Purdy with a wave as he continued to stroll. You couldn't find a more pleasant place than Grundy City in the morning sun. It made Mundus feel proud to have such an orderly place to live, where everyone was so polite and agreeable. Gnomes were well known for their agreeableness, likability, and kindness. It made Mundus wonder why there were so many imbalances in other realms, or with other beings. Was not the **CBE** (Contract for all Beings on Earth), created for this very reason – to maintain harmony between all those who shared the Earth? It seemed to Mundus that perhaps Grundusland was an island of balance within a sea of chaos and disorder. Grundusland, no doubt, had changed little from when his father, Burgus, was king; or his father Rufus before him. Anyhow, only the Shining Ones from the First

Realm truly knew how things had been and were going to be.

In his revelry, Mundus hardly noticed that he had turned into Nocker Lane until he saw the sign hanging outside of Churly's Teahouse. The famous Churly's Teahouse of Grundy City, which used to be one of Mundus's favorite hangouts. He wondered how Churly Bender was these days, whether she was still looking like a pumpkin pie. Mundus popped his face through the door of the teahouse and called out Churly's name.

"Is that you, Mundus? I'd recognize your deep voice anywhere. Bring your kingly self inside. Come on, don't stand there in the doorway like a vagagnome!"

Mundus smiled as he stepped inside and greeted a cheerful, comely Churly Bender. Churly was just a few gnome years older than his wife, Hornie Grundy; although she looked like she had eaten enough pumpkin pies for all three of them!

"Are you on your own, Mundus? Where is the darling Hornie? I hope you've not got her collecting wood, you cheeky smecker!" she said.

"Ohh, no. Don't you fear, Churly, our dear Hornie is happier than a woodchuck in chucked wood. She's in the garden pruning her flowers, and no doubt enjoying the peace and quiet."

"Lucky for you your wife knows how to enjoy peace. Otherwise, you'd have a lot more things on your kingly plate to look after other than chasing rubber-bellied goblins," remarked Churly. Mundus laughed and slapped Churly warmly on her shoulder. He also thought this last remark a little ironic considering Churly would win a prize in any gnome belly competition. "Well, sit yourself down,

Mundus, and I'll bring over a steaming hot pot of fresh Nettle tea, with a homemade pumpkin muffin."

Mundus sat at one of the tables and looked across the teashop. He remembered how he had spent so many days here drinking tea, chatting, and debating as a young carefree gnome. Now those days were gone, and responsibility rested on Mundus's shoulders. The wooden arches of the teashop had supported this establishment for many an age; so too would the shoulders of the Grundy family, thought Mundus. His wistful thoughts turned a quick moment to his son, Fergus, and what he might be up to right now. His unknown whereabouts had troubled Hornie and Mundus for many a gnome year. Yet Veeza, the sun deva, had always assured them not to worry. This was the only thing that kept them at peace, knowing that those of the higher realms had things in perspective.

Over at another table in the teahouse Mundus saw that Dr. Dundus, the gnome doctor and physician, was chatting with Welma Wurdy, the famous and greatest mud-ball thrower in all Grundusland. No doubt they were discussing muscle tension, diet, or something similar. It was all Welma talked about – physical gnome fitness. Welma could lift two gnomes with just one hand. She would be perfect for the GRALE team if only she was interested.

At another table sat Mooley Myrkle, the elder female political analyst, expert on gnomocracy, and advisor to Mundus. Mooley was busy scribbling some notes on a scroll of paper. When she looked up and noticed Mundus, she gave him a nod of recognition and a half-smile and returned to her notes. The hot nettle tea arrived, and Mundus sat back and took a few moments to relax. Grundy City was a special place to be – and he hoped things would not change any time soon.

*****

Elsewhere in Grundy City, Baga Gheet and Serly Frundy were taking a private stroll amongst the tree-lined paths of Pimple Tree Park. Wobin, the big blue shorthair cat, was prowling in the bushes, keeping very close to Serly. The city's main park was popular with young gnomes – especially gnome couples – who loved to stroll around its little lakes and ponds. Often in the warm periods the young gnomes would go swimming and rafting on the largest lake. Now the park was relatively quiet. Most gnomes were busy with their assigned activities. The very young ones would be either in learning groups around the city or practicing woodchuck skills in the forest. It was the perfect time, and place, for what Baga Gheet had in mind.

Baga suggested to Serly that they sit down on one of the benches under the trees. Baga's slightly rounded, youthful face made him look younger than his 399 gnome years. Knowing that Serly was a younger 333 gnome years made Baga feel a little hesitant over his next step. He looked coyly into Serly's pretty face as her long blonde hair partly covered her piercing eyes.

"You're so gnome-pretty," he said a little bashfully. He felt the cheeks of his bearded face glow red.

Serly smiled and reached to squeeze his cheek. "And you, my gnomie Baga Gheet, are so woodchuck-tastic."

Baga tried to hide his embarrassment and glee, yet it was impossible to shield his radiance. "You make me such a better woodchuck," admitted Baga shyly.

Baga and Serly chuckled together like little gnomies. Then Baga reached inside his pocket and brought out a wooden bracelet carved from the root of the *forbiz* tree. The *forbiz* tree only grew in one corner of Grundusland forest, and its roots were known to provide great nutrients for health. For this reason, the roots were also used in sacred rituals of gnome-bonding. Baga held out the bracelet to Serly and, getting onto one gnome-knee, looked unblinking into her eyes.

"I would like very much for you to become my gnome life-partner. Would you accept this bracelet as a sign of our gnomegagement?"

Serly pulled back slightly in surprise, and Wobin purred uneasily beside her. She had not been expecting the seriousness of Baga's affections for her. She was deeply moved, and her little gnomie heart pounded fiercely inside her chest. She was feeling so many emotions and sensations all at once.

"Oh, Baga, you sweetest woodchuck! This is so unexpected – and delightful. Yet...I need you to know that..."

Back at Grundy Castle... Mundus had rushed home as fast as he could as soon as he had received the message from Spritely Neem. He was right to think that the peace and quiet was too good a thing to last! Yet this was something totally new and unheard of. In all his years as King of Grundusland, Mundus had never been summoned to such a meeting before. The heart in his body was beating like a boxing glove. He almost ran into the shining essence of Veeza as he entered the Council Chambers. Her shining presence illuminated the grand room, and her warmth helped Mundus to relax whilst he regained his breath. Just above him hovered Spritely in an ultramarine blue jumpsuit.

"Sorry to make you hurry, Mundus. I felt it was important enough for this not to wait," said Veeza in her calm, soothing voice. "The Elvin Lords have not had reason to come to you before, and nor to your father, Burgus. The last time they presented themselves to a Grundy king was to your grandfather Rufus."

"But...but, I've never heard of the Elvin Lords," stammered Mundus.

"They are rarely present in the Second or Third Realms, preferring to remain active in the First Realm. Like me, they are emissaries of the Shining Ones. However, their work is different from my own. They belong to the inner circle that maintains the cohesion and development of the Three Realms. Other than that, their presence and function is seldom talked about. Your grandfather Rufus would not have discussed openly of their meeting. There must be something serious happening for them to ask for your presence."

Mundus gulped. "When are they coming? How shall we greet them? Do I have time to call a council meeting?"

"This meeting does not require any ceremony. Nor is it for anyone other than yourself. I have been instructed to ask that you go alone to your private quarters. The Elvin Lords will speak with you there." Veeza's soft glow and warmth slowly faded, until Mundus could hear only the slight buzzing of Spritely hovering near his ear.

"Well, I need to go and meet our guests. Perhaps you should wait here, Spritely." Spritely darted away as Mundus followed the steps leading up to his private quarters. When he entered his study, he saw a blue shimmering light beside his desk. He approached slowly and respectfully, not sure what to do or say. As he came closer, the blue light materialized into a thin male figure, with a gentle pale face and long blond hair.

"Greetings, Mundus Grundy, King of Grundusland. My name is Johan, and I am one of the Elvin Lords – we who act as emissaries on behalf of the Shining Ones. I come before you as a hologram of my real self, as I am in the First Realm. I present myself in Grundusland of the Second Realm as your honored guest."

The figure of Johan bowed. He was, suspected Mundus, smaller in the hologram than his actual size; yet still tall in comparison to himself. Johan appeared dressed in a blue one-piece costume. He stood straight, yet with a look that made Mundus feel at ease. Mundus instinctively knew right away that Johan represented a positive, strong energy.

"It is a great honor to receive your presence, Johan of the Elvin Lords, emissary of the Shining Ones. My home is your home." Mundus bowed respectfully. Gnomes valued the function and roles of those in service to the Shining Ones – and all those in service to the realms of the Earth. Was it not the gnomes, after all, who had faithfully maintained the **CBE** throughout all this time? The gnomes had always offered their unconditional service, without question, to the greater good. And now, Mundus sensed that gnome-service was to be called upon in an even greater way.

"Your graciousness and hospitality are greatly appreciated and understood, Mundus Grundy. We of the Elvin Lords salute you gnomes for all you have done. We are in gratitude to your service and regard you as our family. Now, we must speak of matters that are causing some disturbance."

"The goblins?" Mundus shook his head. He knew very well it was something to do with the goblins. Really, these things had just been waiting to happen; and recently Mundus felt that something was coming down the line.

"Yes, Mundus Grundy, it concerns the recent activity of the goblins. These creatures represent a force – an energy – in Nature that serves a specific purpose. You see, even Nature herself requires chaotic events. Like whirlpools of erratic energy, such moments help the Earth to recalibrate the matrix of the Three Realms. Without this disturbance in the system, there is not sufficient energy to catalyze a recalibration. Nothing remains static, my friend. Balance and harmony are an ongoing struggle – there is never a moment without movement."

"Are we gnomes not static in all this?" asked Mundus.

"As I have said, nothing is static in this realm, nor in any of the realms. Stasis only leads to decay. Periods of uncertainty lead to moments of developmental potential. You gnomes represent a balancing function – yet you yourselves are never without movement or change."

Mundus scratched his beard and thought this over. "So," he said after a short pause, "we have now come to such a moment of…what did you call it – recalibration?"

"That is correct," replied the hologram that was Johan. "New forces are arising, both in the Second and the Third Realms. The goblins that remain with you here in the Second Realm have reorganized themselves into a low-functioning social order based on a primitive philosophy and belief system. Such ideas create, and have always created, unpleasant outcomes. However, the energy released by this initial fervor has creative use within the realm. That is, before it solidifies into a rigid system. This initial energy release will cause some disruption and disturbance within the Second Realm. This is coming shortly, and the gnomes must be prepared for this. Do not think that these disruptions are traumatic or unnecessary. You must consider them as part of a developmental movement within the realm. However, there has not been

160

anything like what is coming for a long, long time in this realm. You need to be prepared for the disturbance that is to come. You, Mundus Grundy, must hold out and rally the gnomes to balance this disruptive force. You will, as ever, have our support."

Mundus gulped for a second time. He knew this was serious, and life in Grundy City might never be as peaceful again.

"And this is everything?" As soon as Mundus had said that the image of Farnuk Tam suddenly flashed into his mind. "Oh no!"

"That is not all, Mundus Grundy. There is the matter of Farnuk Tam. We are aware that he is now in the Third Realm. We know roughly his whereabouts."

"And you'd like us gnomes to go in and fetch him out – to do a goblin retrieval job?"

"Not at all – quite the opposite. We wish for Farnuk Tam to remain in the Third Realm."

At this news Mundus's eyebrows went up, and he let out an accidental huff. "Well, that's a new one for us gnomes. What's the plan with Farnuk?"

"The plan, as you call it, is the necessity to leave Farnuk Tam within the Third Realm in order to be yet another catalyst for change."

"And what change is that – the opening of a Farnuk Tam chain of pizza restaurants?" Mundus chuckled at the thought.

"Not quite, Mundus Grundy." Mundus was sure he saw a slight flicker of a smile on the hologram's face. "The energy matrix of the Third Realm requires a slight adjustment. We believe that Farnuk, eventually, will assist in this. This shift, we hope, will positively affect the receiving apparatus of those creatures in the Third Realm, specifically the humans. That is, a change within their brain functioning."

"Wooh! This does sound like a big plan."

"Yes, Mundus Grundy. And this is where you and the gnomes come in."

"It is?" Mundus stood up straight and was all serious again – very gnome-serious.

"Yes. Farnuk Tam has befriended a young boy in the Third Realm. His intentions are not positively aligned. As an Elvin Lord, and as an emissary of the Shining Ones, we are asking the gnomes to also enter the Third Realm for an indefinite period of time. You are also to befriend a young human person, or persons."

"Just the young persons? Why not any of the older big fellows too?"

"Not yet. Not until there has been some energetic adjustment on the matrix to affect human brain functioning. Only the young ones have minds flexible enough to accept the reality of your existence, and to be of help. Older human minds, unfortunately, tend to freeze into rigid patterns. Younger minds will be the ones willing to assist us in the matter of the Three Realms."

"And the plan, once we are there?"

"You are to bide your time. The plan as to what to do will unfold in accordance with events, as is natural. You will know what to do when the moment comes. You must choose only a few trusted and capable gnomes to enter the Third Realm. We shall remove the Protection Protocol from them so they will be immune from the old law and will not turn to stone on human sight. The rest of you will remain here to deal with the coming disturbances in the Second Realm. A period of great change is coming. The gnomes must be ready for this."

"Yes, Johan. You can tell the Elvin Lords, and the Shining Ones, that Mundus Grundy, and the gnomes of Grundusland, are at your service – ready and willing!"

"Thank you, Mundus Grundy, King of Grundusland. We honor your presence. We shall send word shortly – be prepared." Johan bowed, and his holographic image flickered into emptiness.

Mundus flopped down on a chair in the study, as if exhausted from the information.

Shortly, Mundus left his rooms and walked pensively in the direction of the castle kitchen where he knew he would find his wife. Hornie Grundy was stirring a pot of hot vegetable stew as Mundus entered. Mundus gave her a warm gnomie smile and put his arms upon her shoulders.

"I gnome-you so much, my dear," he whispered quietly.

Hornie smiled as she continued to stir the pot. "I know, my dear woodchuck. And being king of Grundusland, you have many more things than me to look after," she replied as if knowing, or feeling, what Mundus could not speak of.

"Yes, indeed, there is so much more on the horizon. Great change is coming…inevitable change like never before. Perhaps the Earth herself will shake. So, Hornie my gnomie, give me a big bowl of that top-tasty stew of yours!"

Somewhere in Pimple Tree Park..."Yeoooowwww," screamed a funny looking Baga Gheet as he scampered along the tree-lined paths. His glittering rounded face looked as if it was going to explode into a rainbow supergnoma. Behind him ran a big blue pudgy cat, meowing and mewing. Then, without warning, he leaped into the lake. "Yeeehaaaa!"

Until next time ...

APPENDIX 1
EXTRACTS FROM THE ETHERIC ANNUALS

"…The Earth exists, yet it doesn't exist in the way that humans think it does. The Earth really exists in three places at once. Or rather, to be more exact, it exists in three different realms simultaneously. All the Three Realms are in the same place. That is, they share the same 'space' – it's just that they vibrate differently. What you see depends on what level *you* are vibrating at…"

"…The Three Realms were vibrationally created upon the Earth by the Shining Ones after a spewd of goblins ran amok over the planet in the early days and putting everything out of balance. They knocked the Earth so out of synch that it fell to one side into a 23.5 degree slant. Now the Earth has an awkward little wobble that messed up the Shining One's plans for its development. It was said that they were very, very peeved about that. So, they decided that the Earth should not exist in just one place – or dimension – but three. The Shining Ones separated the earthly domain into three dimensional realms. That was before the humans arrived. All the inhabitants of the Second Realm were initially allowed to visit Third Realm Earth, so long as they behaved themselves. In the old days there was a contract – known as the *Contract for all Beings on Earth* (**CBE**) – which was signed by all parties to work together for the maintenance of the Earth. Yet the humans soon forgot this contract, neglected the **CBE**, and then they soon forgot about the existence of their 'little helpers' – the gnomes, goblins, fairies, sprites, devas, etc. Then only fragments of stories, myths, grandmothers' tales, and rumors existed in some places, passed down through the generations as bedtime stories. Yet the gnomes, especially, never forgot their contract and continue to this day to work to maintain and look after the Earth…"

"…Goblins have always been a pesky problem. They continued to get loose in the Third Realm, creating havoc and making a mess of things. They once turned up at Stonehenge in a frivolous manner and started to rearrange the stones – they've remained that way ever since! It is also said – in fairy folklore – that a goblin rebel by the name of Kaufuk Tam actually stole the British Royal Family's jewels from the Tower of London, and that the royal dudes themselves were so embarrassed that instead of making the theft public they went and replaced them with fake jewels. This Kaufuk Tam was also said to have been the one responsible for persuading Guy Fawkes to instigate the Gunpowder plot against the British parliament in 1605 H.E.T. (Human Earth Time). Another sticky tale (otherwise known as 'Goblin Truths') is that this very same Kaufuk Tam managed to weasel his way into persuading a young, confused human big fellow into assassinating the Archduke Franz Ferdinand of Austria, thus kick starting World War 1. These, however, are just mainly goblin tales that get bragged about by goblins with puffy-out chests trying to pretend they're the next best thing after swamp slime…"

"…Mundus Grundy inherited the Kingdom of Grundusland from his father, who inherited it from his father, who inherited it from his father…etc. Well, that's basically how the law of Gnome-Inheritance (**GI**) works.

And Grundusland is where all the gnomes of the Second Realm live. And the Third Realm is where the humans live, in their forgetful little bubble…"

APPENDIX 2
BOGGLE:
Book Of Gnomes – Gnome Life and Experience

Items include:

BIG FELLOW – a human being of the Third Realm

CBE – Contract for all Beings on Earth

EGM – Executive Gnome Meeting

GI – the law of Gnome Inheritance

GNOME-HEAD – a gnome idiot

GNOMOCRACY – the open style democracy as practiced by gnomes

GPS – Gnome Positioning System

GRALE – Gnome Rescue and Liberation Expedition (known also as a 'Holy Grale')

GRODA – Gnome Rule Of Direct Action

GRUNDUSLAND ANTHEM – usually sang at important gnome gatherings (such as at the **EGM**)

GWID law – Gnome When In Doubt law

HOG – Holy Oath of a Gnome

HUFFALOT – a miserable gnome

HURDY-GURDY – a gnome working song for fixing energy disturbances

LRG – Light Reflecting Goggles

MATRIGNOME – a silver-colored instrument for measuring energy balance

NOBBY-GNOMES – what gnomes say when playing tricks/teasing

SMECKER – what gnomes say when playing tricks/teasing

STONE-GNOME – a gnome caught/seen by humans and turned into stone

www.ingramcontent.com/pod-product-compliance
Lightning Source LLC
Chambersburg PA
CBHW061448210726
48287CB00007B/2413